Daisy

Jones

Daisy Jones

Mack Mama

PRODIGY GOLD BOOKS

PHILADELPHIA * LOS ANGELES

PRODIGY
GOLDBOOKS

MACK MAMA

A Prodigy Gold Book

Prodigy Gold E-book edition / May 2018

Prodigy Gold Paperback edition / May 2018

Library of Congress Catalog Card Number: 2017954346

Website: http://www.prodigygoldbooks.com

Booking info for speaking engagements, book signings, or performances
contact mackmama1@gmail.com

Twitter: @mackmama @prodigygoldbks

Instagram: @iammackmama @prodigygoldbooks

ISBN 978-1-939665-32-4

Published simultaneously in the US and Canada

PRINTED IN THE UNITED STATES OF AMERICA

Dedication

I dedicate this book to my daughter Velvet G. Washington. All my energy is focused on earning your respect and admiration.

I love you and I want you to know that your mom will never stop reaching for the stars, my entire reason for wanting a great life is so I can provide you with the best education, and a wonderful childhood. I want you to be so much more than I am or Daisy Jones.

To all the young girls in the world who think that using their bodies and physical attributes will "put them on," you will discover through reading Daisy Jones that being a gold digger 'ain't what you think. I dedicate this story to you.

Daisy

Jones

CHAPTER 1

"Bitch, where my thongs at?" yelled Daisy, startling her best friend, Anjel, out of her sleep. "Wake up, hoe, and help me find my rhinestone Victoria Secret thongs. I just bought them and I hope you didn't put your big ass in them," ranted Daisy as she tore up her panty drawer, searching for her thongs.

"Leave me, 'lone beech, I just got to sleep. I've been twirling my ass all night at Magic's and you bothering me 'bout a funky-ass thong. Beech, pleez," said Anjel in her thick southern accent.

Daisy giggled and continued to look for her sexy thongs. She had a hot date with the richest dude in Atlanta and she had to have on her diamond-studded thongs. They were special because they were shaped like a daisy flower complete with the yellow colored rhinestone in the center of the flower. She had the cutest hip-hugging jeans that matched the thongs. The jeans had a hand-drawn rose with ruby red stones embellishing the design down the front of the right leg. She planned to rock a white push up bra with cute little daisy's decorating the satin finish with the outfit.

Daisy had luscious 36C's and she planned to let her girls show. She wasn't going to cover up her sexy bra with a shirt, not with her washboard flat stomach. Buffie the body had nothing on Daisy Jones, her measurements were 36, 26, 42 and she had a heart-shaped ass that stopped traffic. She was definitely stacking and she knew it and used her sexy frame to her advantage. That night she was going out with Young Chio, the hottest rapper on the market representing the dirty south. Daisy had been scheming on him for months and she finally managed to be featured in his latest video. That was all it took for him to notice her. Daisy owed it all to her best friend Anjel, who was an exotic dancer at Magic City, the most popular strip club in Atlanta. It was well known that Magic's had the finest women in the south dancing there. When rappers needed some bootilicious eye candy, that's where they went.

Daisy didn't work there, but Anjel would holla at her when they wanted girls for videos, so when Anjel called Daisy and told her about Chio's video Daisy was ecstatic. She had been trying to get at Young Chio for a minute. She had just left *Star Status Styles* her favorite beauty salon and one of the hottest shops around. All the girls from Housewives of Atlanta reality show went there and any given day you could bump into a celebrity. Fresh from a spa treatment she rushed to the mansion in Decatur, Georgia where the video was being shot. Daisy knew the directions by heart because all the entertainers used different mansions in that area for their videos. The beautiful estates were rented and showcased in videos and on MTV Cribs. Daisy stayed abreast of all the hot spots always on the hunt for a potential "vic" (victim) a baller, hot boy or her personal favorite, a rapper. Rappers were so dumb it wasn't funny. They were all the same: self-absorbed, arrogant, and a sucker for a fat ass. Not necessarily a pretty face, but if you had a big booty and juicy tits you could manipulate the best of them. All it took was a little game, which Daisy Jones had plenty of. She played dumb, but whoever fell for that act was a goner. All she had to do was flash her big green eyes, which to her benefit were the real deal. When a guy asked her if she had contacts she would smile seductively and purr "Everything on Daisy Jones is real, baby." That was her slogan guaranteed to wrap any man around her finger, from the play it cool baller that normally acted aloof, to the over-anxious playa whose only agenda was to get into her panties.

They all wanted a piece of Daisy and she knew how to benefit from their lust. What made her unique was the fact that as sexy and provocative as she appeared she was still a virgin. That was what made her so special, she was only sixteen, but she was extremely mature and intelligent enough to know the value of her virginity. She had zero tolerance for a cheap nigga or a broke one. Her mama instilled gold digger values in her from an early age. Mama Jones also made her realize that holding out and not giving away her most prized possession was the key to the goldmine.

Daisy watched her mother make the mistake of getting knocked up six times and vowed she would never allow the possibility of an accident. No man was going to pump his load in her and mess up her goldmine. "No babies for Daisy" was her motto and she stood by it. On the other hand, she knew she had to give something up eventually, especially when the gifts were lavish. The likelihood of a man continuing to spoil her if she didn't put up something was very rare. There were too many other girls around willing to skeez and please. So she practiced and perfected the art of oral sex. She could suck a cock better than the infamous *Super Head* and *Heather Hunter* combined. She learned her techniques from hours of watching and studying Porn DVDs. She practiced on pop bottles and bananas and mastered deep-throating on a green, nine-inch long plantain.

She sucked a BMW out of her last conquest a young baller named, Anthony Davis. He signed to the NBA for a record-breaking fifty million, seven-year deal and Daisy met him two weeks after he signed his deal. Within a month she had him wrapped around her little pinky. He was so caught up in her magnificent head game that he bought her a two passenger, custom painted, pink BMW with a matching pink *Chanel* bag. The car was hot and she had her eye on the purse for a while. It was an exclusive piece and very hard to obtain.

The waiting list was infinite but Anthony made it happen. His manager called Chanel's corporate office and had two of the treasured bags shipped to him for the whopping cost of seven thousand. He gave one to Daisy and sent one to his mom.

Daisy loved a powerful man that called the shots. Nothing made her mouth water more. After she made sure that her Beemer was in her name and fully paid for she decided to end the affair. The poor guy was devastated. He really thought she loved him. He soon discovered that Daisy was only sixteen and while he was only twenty-five, he was definitely sleeping with a minor, a fact that she decided to point out to him when he kept pushing her to have sex with him.

That was a major turn off. She figured he should have been satisfied with the blazing oral she gave him. She even gave him a treat the night he surprised her with the car—she swallowed. She only drank when there was "major bank" another motto she lived by. But that wasn't good enough for him. He had to mess up everything up by annoying her for some pussycat.

"Stop nigga, I told you I'm a virgin. *Damnnnnn*," screamed Daisy, highly irritated.

"But, ma, I love you. What a nigga gotta do to show you I'm real? You can trust me. I won't hurt you. As good as I treat you don't I deserve to be your first?" he pleaded with all the sincerity in the world and his best game face.

"Hell No. You ain't worthy just because you gave me that Beamer. I'm supposed to hop on your dick?" before he could reply she yelled

"Hell no. I ain't no ho. I'm Daisy Jones, the only chick that you ain't never gonna bone." She was so angry she bust a rhyme on his ass.

Anthony was flabbergasted. He wanted to smack the shit out of her for dissing him like that. No chick had ever talked to him with such blatant disrespect.

Even before he signed his deal he was very popular with the ladies. He wasn't an ugly dude. At least he didn't think so. He was 6'9", dark skinned, African black, as his homies like to call him when they playfully traded insults. It didn't bother him because he had a supersized twelve-inch dick that was just as black and the ladies loved it. He knew if he could get Daisy to let him hit it one time she would be sprung and all his.

He felt so hopeless because he had no control over her and she had him open off her phenomenal oral sex. Emotionally and physically she sucked him into submission. He had received head from the best freaks around, but no one made him feel like Daisy Jones. She brought the bitch out of him when she breathed on his manhood. "Damn," he said. "If I didn't love this bitch, I would shit on her." But, he knew, he would never diss her. She had him fucked up.

"Anthony, I have something to tell you." Daisy's tone changed dramatically. She was in serious mode.

Oh no, he thought "Don't tell me this chick is sick and that's why she won't let me hit it."

"What's up ma? You can talk to me about anything," he assured her, silently praying he couldn't catch the monster from her mouth.

"I'm only sixteen," declared Daisy proudly with no shame in her game.

"Huh?" Anthony was dumbfounded. He couldn't believe this bombshell that had been sucking his dick like a professional for the last four weeks was only a kid. "Cut the jokes Daisy" he willed her to admit that she was just playing so his heart could start beating again.

"It's no joke honey, I'm sorry, but I'm afraid I'm underage and it's illegal to fuck me," she stated bluntly. "Matter fact sucking you off is a major sodomy no-no, but I won't tell if you won't," she teased evilly. She wanted Anthony to shit his pants thinking about losing his million-dollar endorsement deals and the headlines in the newspaper if the media got a whiff off his relationship with an underage girl. She could see the headline: *Anthony Davis Arrested for Statutory Rape of a Minor. Ole boy would be ruined*, she thought. *Oh well.*

"Daisy—Man why didn't you tell me your age in the beginning?" he whined agitated with her for the deception.

"You didn't ask me," she replied cockily.

"I have to stop seeing you ma. I can't let this ruin my career I will be in serious trouble." Anthony thought about the Kobe Bryant incident and knew that the NBA had zero tolerance for any allegations or mentions of foul play, period. "As much as I dig you I have to end this," he told her with genuine regret. He really cared about her but not enough to destroy his career.

"Sure no problem playa, since you "dig" me as you put it, DIG in your stash and give me some money. cuz if you think your gonna use me up like a washrag then hang me out to dry you got Daisy Jones twisted." She replied coldly. Who did this

7

dude think he was dealing with? He had just finished professing his love for her then as soon as he found out her age his "love" turned to "dig". She hated fake ass men but she had a trick for his ass, she was going to make him pay like he weighed to end their little illegal affair.

"You fucking little whore. You played me didn't you?" he roared, enraged at her as the realization hit him that she played him. She was scheming on him from the very beginning.

"If I was you I would watch my tone and choose your words carefully because I'm far from a whore baby, I'm a virgin who just screwed you. Now, I know you keep a stash in your safe in your bedroom. Twenty thousand oughta do it. I'll put it up for my college fund. We'll call it a donation," said Daisy. "Let's go." She giggled as he stormed to his bedroom to get her money. Daisy chuckled as she recalled the last night with ole Anthony.

She went on a hell of a shopping spree after that sting, so when Anjel called about the shoot Daisy packed her garment bag full of designer pieces and headed out to steal the spotlight from every video vixen there.

* * *

When she arrived the circular driveway was packed with luxury vehicles. There were custom and chromed out 404 rims on every type of car imaginable Hummers, Maybach's and the Bentley GTC convertible that she loved. She hoped to trade her

BMW in for one of those babies as soon as she bagged Young Chio. She probably wouldn't even need to trade in her two-seater she would simply get him to buy her the Bentley. She also needed her own house. She still lived at home with her mama and all her little sisters and brothers, which was a drag. She needed to score a major baller so she could do it big and move out of her mama's house.

"Oooh, there he go," she gushed to herself when she spotted Young Chio. That boy was a superstar originally from Stone Mountain, Georgia, but he screamed ATL like he was homegrown. It was so popular to rep Atlanta ever since Jermaine Dupree the superstar producer that calls himself the mayor of Atlanta put the city on the map it was so cool to be from Hotlanta. Young Chio's hit single "Tata Bounce" was blaring and all the girls were bouncing their Tata's to the beat and trying to upstage each other. Daisy personally thought the song was hilarious and watching the girls with their silicone filled breasts battle each other was hysterical. She felt wonderful as she strutted towards the pool in her tight fitted Baby Phat T-shirt displaying her perky 36's. They were grapefruit round and soft to the touch, an obvious indicator of the real thing. It was something about the natural bounce she possessed that drove the men wild. So many of the scantily clad girls' breasts were so hard they looked like they were in physical pain.

Daisy knew all eyes were on her and she loved it, she was the new fish on the set. She had only been to one other video shoot and that was for R&B singing sensation *Usher*. She had been picked to frolic around in a hot tub with him and another girl, while he serenaded the camera. She had fun but couldn't pull him because his woman was on the scene cockblocking. The chick wouldn't give her a minute to mesmerize him with her eyes. That wasn't going to happen again, vowed Daisy. She was going to bag Chio if it was the last thing she did.

I'm so glad I didn't wear a bra underneath this T-shirt, she thought as she imagined sitting on Young Chio's face so her nipples could get hard. She was so voluptuous that she didn't need to put on any fancy clothes. A simple baby tee and hip hugger jeans were all it took to entice and stand out. She knew all the girls would be half-naked so she wanted to leave something to his imagination. She allowed a slither of skin to peak out just inches away from her spine and her booty crack. She knew her ass was the main attraction. She had removed her panties as soon as she got the call from Anjel.

Daisy had a special switch she perfected. She jiggled each ass cheek sensually as she strutted in her stilettos. She was 5'7" without heels, so the six-inches gave her the length of a supermodel. She resembled Tyra Banks without the high forehead, but they shared the same hazel green eyes and love for long hair, except Daisy didn't wear weaves. She took after her father's genes. He was a white man and although she never met him, her mama told her she looked just like him. She had her mama's deep chocolate complexion with thick long jet black curly hair, and her exotic eyes completed her sultry look. People often thought she was Caribbean, all Daisy knew was she drove men and some women crazy. "Big tits, small waist, fat ass, sweet taste, all that plus a pretty face ooh wee she was dat bitch," she giggled to herself.

"Damn, dawg, who that fine bitch walkin' this way?" Young Chio asked the director of his video. He was grinning so hard his diamond encrusted platinum grillz were blinding Ted Bond, the popular young Caucasian director.

"Never saw her before," replied Ted, checking Daisy out from head to toe "But she is a fine ass hoe, my nigga," he said using ebonics and a fake wanna be down swagger.

"nigga, what makes you think you can call my beech a hoe? Stay in your place, white boy and watch who you call a nigga, too. nigga." Barked Chio disgusted at the director's familiarity and fake b-boy swagger. He hated when white folks didn't stay in their place, especially when they pretended to be down and used slang.

"Cool dude, my bad. Let me find out who she is," Ted replied nervously, trying to calm Chio down and remedy the situation. An upset Chio meant a messed up video and he needed this video to be a hit or he wouldn't be hired for the next three videos for the singles Chio was releasing.

As much as he hated to be around these stupid niggas he stayed humble and thought, he needed to keep the checks rolling in.

Ted signaled for his assistant, "Yes, boss?"

"Bring that girl over here, the pretty chocolate one with the tight T-shirt. Chio wants to meet her." Ted ordered his assistant Jay to fetch the girl for Chio. He was used to picking thru the field of pussies for his celebrity clients. They always wanted to sample the beauties that surrounded them in their videos.

"I gotcha, no problemmo boss." Jay smiled and hurried off to do his bosses bidding. He loved his job, especially the perks of being around sexy woman all day on video sets. It was a dream position.

"Excuse me sexy, the director would like a word with you. Looks like it's your lucky day sweetheart," he winked at Daisy and licked his lips, appreciating the sexy juice she was dripping. Jay had worked on hundreds of shoots with his boss and he still couldn't believe his luck. He was able to flirt with some of the sexiest women on the planet without getting a drink thrown in his face. The beauties all wanted a chance at stardom and would do anything to anybody to get camera time. Occasionally Jay got lucky if he could convince a new fish that he could "hook her up" with a leading role in a video. He prayed that he could run some game on Daisy. He wanted her bad. *Damn this new fish is fine as hell*, he thought, getting an instant erection. His cock was ready to bust just thinking about how it would feel to place it between her fat butt cheeks. Jay was an ass man. He didn't mind taking it in his own ass once in a while either. Every now and then he would run into a thug rapper that needed his personal assistance. He loved him a homo thug and Atlanta was crawling with them. Jay knew plenty of industry boys who liked to play dirty boy games. "What a life," Jay said, smiling at Daisy.

"OK let's see if it's my lucky day. I sure hope so sweetie," Daisy flirted with Jay making his day. *Lil' creepy*, she thought as she looked Jay up and down with her sexy come-suck-me smile. She was cringing at the sight of him. He was the nerdiest white boy she had ever seen. He had severe acne that didn't make a bit of sense when all he had to do was order *Proactive*. Shit, even P Diddy used the magic pimple remover. *This fool should know about that product, being in the business,* she thought and shook her head. *Nerdy thinks I like him.* She wanted to roll her eyes and suck her teeth at the corny man, but she needed him on her team to get closer to Chio, so she played the game. "What's your name?" asked Daisy feigning interest in him,

"That would be Jay at your service, princess. Whatever you need just holla atcha boy," he smiled with his best B-Boy impression. Daisy smiled and shook her head in bewilderment. *This white boy is crazy*, she thought as she gave him a huge smile.

"You're so cute" she gushed almost laughing out loud at the outlandish lie. She knew she had him when he just nodded with a goofy smile and turned beet red.

"Hey, boss, this gorgeous specimen's name is ahh....What did you say your name was, hon?"

"Daisy Jones, sweetie," replied Daisy, ignoring Jay as she extended her delicate wrist clad with her four-carat diamond tennis bracelet to shake the director's hand. "Please to meet you, Mr. Bond," she purred.

"Call me Ted, babe. Listen, uh…Daisy come with me. Young Chio would like to meet you." Ted leered at Daisy lustfully. He was pleased with how foxy she looked. He knew Chio would keep her around for a while. He led Daisy over to the pool deck where Chio was standing, surrounded by what looked like women from the Miss Black America Pageant.

"Yo, Chio guess who I found to be your leading lady? This pretty flower is named Daisy, you like that?"

"Hell yeah, I likes that. Come here Miss Daisy wit ya bad ass self. Do you wanna be my 'shawty in this here scene?" asked Chio as he undressed her with his eyes from head to toe.

"That's a start baby, but what's up after the scene?" teased Daisy in her sexiest voice. Chio grinned.

"Damn Ted, you picked me a bona fide' stunna this time and 'shawty got game, too. Come over here lil' mama and let me see what' ya working wit'," whooped Chio. He was excited and very animated. He loved to have a good time and was ready to have some fun with Daisy. He knew a fly ass chick when he saw one and this Daisy Jones was a diva. He was used to the finest of women all day, every day but he was also tired of the same old shit. He had women all colors shapes and sizes, but Daisy seemed different she looked so exotic with her green eyes and damn if her weave didn't look real, he mused. "Excuse me, ladies, I have to get my 'shawty ready for this shot," Chio dismissed the flock of chickens clucking for his attention. Daisy could have leaped for joy. This was going to be easier than she thought. He had dissed all the girls at the video shoot for her.

She beamed with pride and satisfaction as the girls sulked away shooting daggers at her. *Beat it*, she thought. *Poof be gone. It's time for me and my man to get to know each other.*

"So, Daisy show me what you working wit. I need to see how you bounce those big juicy tata's to my song," said Young Chio. Daisy smiled and licked her lips as she spread her legs and started bouncing to the beat of his hit single, she rubbed her Tata's and bounced them while poppin' her ass. She rapped along to the song spitting the lyrics word for word.

Bounce those Tata's mommie
Pop that booty climb me
Ride this pony
Do it like you own me
I like 'em when they're real not phony
Bounce 'em like a yo-yo
Strip for your boy young Chio

She bounced and performed popping her ass and tits to the beat. Chio was mesmerized. Daisy had him right where she wanted him, that day.

She smiled at the memory of their first meeting. She strutted over to her man. They had been dating for several weeks and were inseparable since the video shoot.

"Girl you look sexy as hell. Whoo wee. Turn around, let me see that ass full circle," yelled Chio, laughing like a hyena. He smiled so hard, his platinum grillz looked like they were going to pop out of his mouth.

"Thank you, boo. You look good, too." Daisy returned the compliment and she meant it. Although he was loud as hell and didn't have an ounce of class. He was so rich all that other shit was negotiable. She dripped in her thongs when she looked at him and he wasn't a handsome guy, but he worked out and was chiseled to perfection. His body resembled the boxer, Floyd Mayweather Jr's He had a six pack, looking like a washboard. Daisy loved a man that took care of his body. The only thing that turned her off was his teeth. His platinum grillz annoyed her. She couldn't appreciate the style. It was a southern thing and by right being a southern girl she should love them but the thought of kissing him with all that junk in his mouth turned her stomach.

She didn't care that the diamonds engraved in the grillz were worth 100,000 they just didn't appeal to her. To top his outrageous personality he had blond long dreads, he was dark skinned and his blond dreads made him look crazy but they fit him to a tee.

"Daisy Jones I love them thongs."

"Now you know you dead wrong."

"Make a nigga bone grow long."

"Big black like he king kong."

"OUUU WEEE, that's a hit," Chio whooped. He was pleased with his impromptu freestyle.

"You so crazy Chio, but that did sound crunk. I love when you freestyle," Daisy said, giggling.

"I'm the king baby. Stick wit' ya boy and you can be my queen." Chio winked and was interrupted by his cell phone. Daisy smiled as he leaned on his black Rolls Royce Phantom and started talking loudly to his producer. She was ecstatic that she succeeded with her mission to get with the hottest rapper on the map and damn if she didn't do it. The next step was to get him to fall in love with her, which shouldn't be hard. She just had to convince him to be patient, because rich or not he was not screwing her. Even if he did have his own very successful million dollar Record Label. So what if his clothing line was the hottest urban apparel on the market, surpassing Jay-Z's Rocawear brand and second to Sean John's line. OK, realistically if he pressured her to give up her goldmine she would probably relent but he had to marry her straight up. Fuck that. She wanted it all and she wouldn't settle for less. It was the small matter of her age standing in the way so she decided to come clean.

"Come on, lil' mama, where you wanna eat at?" asked Chio, clicking off his phone.

"Let's go to Babalu's over in Glenwood Park."

Sean Paul from the rap group the Young Bloodz owned the popular Cuban restaurant. It was Daisy's favorite.

"I need to tell you something before we leave, baby." Daisy gazed at him with her hazel eyes.

"What is it baby girl? You can holla at ya boy 'bout anything," Young Chio assured her with a look of concern.

"Well." Daisy took a deep dramatic breath and exhaled slowly causing her breast to pop out slightly from her bra. Chio couldn't take his eyes off of her juicy tatas. He loved breasts and Daisy had a set of beauties. He wanted to know if they were real because they looked too perfect.

"Before you say anything let me guess? Your 'tata's are fake and you just had to let me know," he joked with a straight face, that he couldn't keep from cracking a smile.

"You so silly. For your information everything on Daisy Jones is real," She replied sassily, pretending to roll her eyes.

"Ooh, where? Lemme see," said Chio gleefully, reaching over to squeeze her breast. "Stop fool you're crazy," Daisy swatted his hand laughing at his outrageous antics.

"Seriously, Chio, I need you to know something before we leave," she paused and blurted out "I'm a virgin."

"You a what? Get the hell out of here, girl." Chio looked at her like she was a two-headed alien.

"That's what I had to tell you, I don't want you to expect nothing you ain't getting," she broke it down primly. "I know how to please my man in other ways, but I'm saving my virginity for my future husband," she stated coyly and gazed at him with an innocent expression.

She decided to save the age part for later. She wanted to take it one step at a time. She didn't want to scare him off and telling him he couldn't get any pussy was enough to make him hit the road. She knew she offered a challenge and he was going to take the bait. Every man wants to be the first one to bed a girl, especially if she looks like Daisy Jones.

"Whoa girl, that's some deep shit, you caught a nigga off guard, but hell I respect that shit. You the last untapped piece of booty on the planet." He grinned and stared at her like he wanted to eat her alive. "Matter fact, I don't believe that shit. Let me see it," he demanded with a devilish grin on his face. "Make Chio know that shit you kickin' is real. Spread your legs and let me see if you ain't been touched."

"You're so silly. I don't have to lie 'bout no shit like that and I'm not gonna let you treat me like no groupie hoe," replied Daisy with fake indignation. She really didn't mind spreading her legs for him. She knew she had a pretty pussy. It was freshly waxed so all he could do is sniff, taste and put it all in his face. She knew she had to act insulted so he would take her seriously and respect her wishes. One thing for sure and two things for certain, he wasn't going to dismiss her. The chase had just begun.

"No sir, lil mama, I ain't mean to offend you, it's just I never heard that before and I'm amazed that as fine as you are a nigga ain't tore that thang up yet."

"They all try but I want to give the man I marry something special, but," she paused and licked her lips enticingly, "I still know how to please my man if he deserves it," she giggled and tossed her wild mane of curls over her shoulder adjusting her bra and rubbing her breast suggestively. "

"Girl, you something kinda special. Come 'er." With that being said he grabbed her neck gently and gave her the longest French kiss she ever had to endure. After a few seconds of his wet tongue slobbering her down, she couldn't take his Hennessy breath and pushed him away. "Aw dang baby you trying to swallow my tongue?"

"Baby girl, I'm fittin' to swallow ya pussy if it's fresh as I'm iz," cackled Chio quoting the rapper Bow Wow's hit single.

Daisy couldn't stop smiling. She was really digging Young Chio. He was so charming in his loud brash southern way. "So you won't try to pressure me to have sex with you?" she asked him just to make sure.

"Sheeet, Young Chio don't sweat no hoe. Ain't no ass worth seeing popo," he replied sarcastically. "I tell you what." He switched up his tone and became serious, staring directly into Daisy's eyes. "Give me a chance to show you, I'm a different nigga than all those chumps chasing you down for your p-bone."

"My p-bone?"

"Yeah, baby, that cute lil' pussy bone you tryna protect. I'ma keep it real wit' ya. I got a hundred women I can call for sex so I can save you for that lucky dude you marry, but you never know it just might be me," he winked at her and started his Phantom. He put on his CD and rapped along to track ten, *All lips on me*, a racy song, describing the pleasures of every woman on the planet giving him head.

This is going to be so easy, Daisy thought as she slid down into the plush ultra suede bucket seat with Young Chio's name monogrammed on it. She listened to the lyrics of his song and grinned. She knew after her lips touched him it would be a wrap, literally as she wrapped her tongue around his shaft. Oooh, she got wet thinking about it, not yet though, she was gonna make him pay like he weighed first. Especially since he agreed to wait for her p-bone. She giggled as she thought about his nickname for pussy.

"What you over there laughing about?"

"Nothing baby, your song is the bomb and I'm imagining a bunch of girls giving you head," answered Daisy dreamily.

"Oh, you like that shit, huh? That freaky leaky shit turns you on?"

Daisy giggled at Chio's teasing.

"Baby you won't need more than me to fulfill your fantasy. Trust and believe, Daisy Jones is all you need," she purred and leaned over and licked his ear erotically.

This girl is a live one, Chio thought, *an innocent freak*. He couldn't imagine that and he wasn't going to let her go until he found out if her p-bone was really untouched, and if it was true, she was a keeper. He ran his hands over her head and damn if he ain't feel no weave tracks. She really was all natural. Daisy definitely was wifey material fo' sho'.

CHAPTER 2

Remy Ma's song *I'm Conceited* blared from Anjel's phone, startling her out of her sleep. "Holla at me," she drawled still in a semi-conscious stupor.

"Beech, guess where I'm at?" Daisy whispered excitedly on the phone.

"It better be somewhere good hoe, if you waking me up three in the morning," Anjel sucked her teeth as she peeped at her clock.

"Girlll…Chio flew me to Vegas on his private jet and we are checking into the Bellagio," gushed Daisy.

"Beech, you act like you're at one of those marriage drive throughs 'bout to marry dat nigga. I know you ain't wake me up to tell me that?" Anjel feigned anger but she was really happy for her best friend.

"Oh, stop hatin', silly, I just want you to know where I am in case anything jumps off, and for the record when I marry him it damn sure ain't gonna be at some tacky ass marriage chapel in Vegas. Save that shit for Britney Spears silly ass. My baby gonna give me a horse and carriage affair fit for a queen," bragged Daisy.

"I know that's right beech," Anjel chuckled Daisy always knew how to make her laugh. "OK, girl, have fun and pick me up something cute from *Christian Dior* because I know you fittin' to take his rich ass shopping"

"Girl, shut up. He already told me whatever I want I can get. I got you, ooh here he comes. I gotta go," Daisy ended the conversation with an abrupt click.

That damn Daisy is a lucky hoe, Anjel thought as she rolled over and reached for a cigarette from her nightstand. Once she woke up from a deep sleep it was hard to get back into it. She lit her *Newport Light* and took a deep drag as she blew out three quick smoke rings and huffed. Damn, she envied and admired Daisy. She had it all, hot looks, a sexy ass body and she got any man she wanted. She loved her to death but couldn't help feeling slightly jealous.

She laid back on her comfortable pile of goose down pillows and recalled her first encounter with Daisy. They went to grade school together. Anjel was very shy and didn't socialize with the other children in school. She was always a nerdy looking girl. She wore thick bifocal reading glasses and wore her coarse thick hair in two ponytails. She never had nice clothes to wear but she was neat and clean so she didn't mind. That was until she met Daisy Jones.

Daisy strolled into her fifth-grade class looking cute as a button. She resembled a chocolate covered Barbie doll. Anjel never saw a dark skinned girl with such silky curly hair and she had the prettiest green eyes. She was taller than the average fifth grader and very mature. She even had boobs which blew Anjel away because she was flat as a board and was desperate to grow some. Her mother kept telling her she would develop into a beautiful butterfly, but she felt like an ugly caterpillar. When she laid eyes on Daisy she was mesmerized and wanted to be just like her. The teacher introduced her to the class cheerily. "Everybody say hello to your new classmate, Daisy Jones."

"Hello, Daisy," the class droned in unison.

"Sit by me Daisy." shouted the usually quiet Anjel. The entire class spun around in shock and stared at Anjel who had never so much as answered a question in the past. Mrs. Cambry the teacher, smiled and directed Daisy to sit by Anjel she was pleased that the usually shy girl was being friendly. That day Anjel and Daisy became best friends and were inseparable.

Daisy transformed Anjel and helped her convince her mom, to let her put a relaxer in her hair. After weeks of pleading with her mom she finally gave in. "Anjel you is too young to perm your hair. Daisy has natural good hair. You can't be like her. You're gonna mess around and all your hair is gonna fall out," her mother warned.

"Ah mama, no it ain't. Please, I'm tired of my nappy hair. "Anjel nagged, cried and whined until her mother finally gave her the money she needed to buy the relaxer. She raced to the phone to call Daisy. "I'll be right over," replied Daisy. The next day Anjel was transformed.

"Oh, my lawd, I can't believe it. I have long straight hair," said Anjel excitedly.

"I told you that after you relaxed it that your naps would disappear and your hair would stretch longer," said Daisy combing Anjel's hair approvingly. "Now all we have to do is get rid of those ugly glasses and you'll be gorgeous." Before Daisy could finish her sentence Anjel was gone running to her mother's bedroom.

"Ma." yelled Anjel frantically "I need contacts."

Anjel was an only child and although her mother was a single parent she loved her child and wanted to see her happy. It was hard to provide for her, but Barbara-Jean Brown tried to give her Anjel what she could. She was on welfare and had a job paying her off the books. So she had a few extra dollars after she bought her weekly bottle of *Jack Daniels* and her carton of cigarettes for the week. *Shit*, Barbara-Jean thought. Her baby girl deserved to look pretty and feel good about herself. She stroked Anjel's pretty, freshly straightened hair lovingly.

"OK, suga'. Here is a hundred dollars. Go to the mall and get your eyes checked. This should be enough to get you a set of contacts, but no color. You ain't Daisy you have pretty eyes just the way they are and I want you to be yourself, you hear me?" Barbara-Jean didn't want her baby being a follower. She loved Daisy for being a positive influence in her daughter's life. She helped boost Anjel's confidence and self-esteem, but she

25

wanted Anjel to love herself for who she was not who she wanted to be like.

"Yes, mama thanks, I love you." Anjel pecked her quickly on the cheeks and dashed out the door.

Barbara- Jean smiled. She knew how it felt to want to be pretty. She was worn out, tired and appeared to be much older than her 40 years. Drinking and smoking ravaged her once pretty face. She was also very ill and tried to conceal her sickness from her child, but she knew it was time to tell Anjel that she was slowly dying. Barbara-Jean had lung cancer. She had been diagnosed with the disease for six months. She decided that before she let the chemotherapy the doctor suggested make her sicker than she already felt, she would take her chances without it. She was weak all the time and the pain was unbearable. Her only comfort was her Jack Daniels and the poisonous smoke that seemed to calm the pain in her blackened lungs. How ironic that the cause of her ailment was also the cure or so she thought.

Barbara-Jean Brown was dead two months later, leaving Anjel devastated and an orphan. Anjel was twelve years old and all alone. Her mother had no family in Atlanta. She was from North Carolina and was raised in a foster home. Barbara-Jean never told Anjel what happened to her parents. All she knew was Barbara-Jean grew up in foster care. She gave birth to Anjel when she was twenty-eight-years-old. Anjel never knew who her father was. When she questioned her mother she would start crying, which led to her running to the liquor store for a bottle of her beloved Jack Daniels. On her deathbed she broke down and told Anjel that she had been raped and that's how Anjel was conceived. She did not know who Anjel's father was and as far as she was concerned he was a monster.

Tears ran down Anjel's face as she took a deep drag off of her cigarette and recalled the nightmare of her mother's last words. "Anjel you know you're mama's baby right?" Barbara-Jean locked eyes with her oldest daughter as she wiped the tears from her face.

"Yes 'ma'am, I know," Anjel sniffed, weeping in shock over the realization that her beloved mother was dying. Barbara-Jean had deteriorated so rapidly that Anjel knew it would be any day before she passed away. She was crushed and angry at God for allowing her mother to become so sick. What was she going to do without her? She was too young to live alone and therefore Barbara-Jean had to make arrangements with children services to place Anjel in foster care. History would repeat itself. She was raised by foster parents and now so would be Anjel.

"Anjel, I'm going to tell you something that you need to know," Barbara-Jean whispered as she gasped for air, barely managing to talk. "I was raped baby, that's how you came into this world. I don't know who your father is."

Anjel gasped in shock and let out a wounded cry. "Noooo. Ma, why didn't you tell me before?"

"I'm sorry, Anjel. I couldn't bring myself to hurt you like that. I knew you would be upset. I tried to protect you."

Barbara-Jean cried as she delivered the news that she knew would devastate her daughter.

Anjel choked back a sob and jumped out of her bed. She ran to the bathroom and vomited. Every time she let herself think about that awful day she became sick. She splashed her face with cold water—the icy blast helped her clear her head. She plopped on the toilet and scrambled through her basket of cosmetics until she found her stash of weed. She was relieved when she touched her sack of *Mexican Haze*. She ripped open a box of strawberry-flavored Dutch blunts and peeled the cigar open, dumping the guts and filled it with her weed.

Her hands were shaking so bad that she spilled half the buds on her lap. Finally, she got it together and rolled a decent blunt and lit it up. In minutes, her nerves were calmed. She relaxed as she floated, high from the effects of the magic herbs. *Gawd, I am the product of a fucking monster. What kind of freak would force his self on a woman?* she thought. She leaned back and drifted into a troubled sleep.

Barbara-Jean heard heavy footsteps behind her. She glanced over her shoulders and saw a crazed looking man speeding towards her. *Oh shit,* she thought and began running. She tripped and fell and the man descended on her. The lunatic punched her in the face and ripped her skirt off. His brute force dragged her panties off as she screamed and swung her fist at him, but she was no match for the monster. Nothing could stop him from violating her. He bashed her face again and all she could do was take the beating. She spits up the blood that gushed in her mouth from her busted lips. The searing pain that enveloped her body and the burning sensation from her ripped vagina was so horrible she felt like dying. It was all she could do not to faint as he stuck his filthy penis inside of her with no condom. "Gawd help me," she prayed as she endured the evil, barbarous attack'

Anjel jolted out of her nod, nearly falling in the toilet. She was drenched in sweat and hysterical. That was the first time since Barbara Jean's death that she saw her mom in a dream and the first time she saw her father.

CHAPTER 3

"I'm in love with a stripper and she rollin' she rollin'..." Anjel twirled her legs around the pole at Magic's and gyrated her ass to the pulsating beats from her favorite song. It was the anthem for all the exotic dancers at the club. Each of the sexy strippers tried to out-dance one another when the song played. It was a pussy popping, ass ticking, tit rubbing showdown. It got hot and crazy when T-Pain, the rapper that sang the song came in the club. He was treated like a king at Magic City and the place would get out of control. Every girl in the club wanted to be the stripper he was in love with.

Anjel was in her own fantasy world while she twirled around on the stage in her six-inch platform heels. She imagined being the only woman on the planet performing for all her adoring lovers. She was a glorified nymphomaniac—she couldn't get enough of sex. She needed a man to penetrate her and at least pretend that he gave a shit about her. She felt like she didn't deserve love because she was the product of a brutal rape and loved the attention she received when she danced. Dancing was the only time that she felt good about herself. She felt like a celebrity when she was on stage and spared no expense for her costumes.

She wore pieces from Fredericks of Hollywood. She looked hot and knew it. Anjel came a long way from the nappy headed nerd she was in grade school. With the help of her best friend, Daisy, she had matured into a pretty woman. She had grown some tits. They weren't very big, but her B-cups were pretty as hell. She loved her nipples—they stayed hard and were big as peanuts. Men drooled over them—they were her best assets. She was 5'5" with thick, curvaceous legs and a plump booty, but as pretty as she was Anjel felt ugly inside. She knew a rapist's blood ran thru her veins and it disgusted her.

The club's house DJ Bub C threw on Anjel's second favorite song *Rodeo* by Juvenile, the popular New Orleans rapper. It was another ode to the exotic dancers. Anjel rode her pole like a thoroughbred. "Damn, shawty, shake that ass and come ride me like you in a rodeo" A rowdy customer shouted at her. Anjel smiled erotically and granted the request of her steady customer. He was a big spender and she had freaked with him a few times in the infamous champagne room, a section of the club dedicated to the high rollers who wanted privacy with the girls. Basically, anything could pop off in the champagne room, as long as the money kept flowing. Anjel's clients would wait in line to spend thousands with her with no problem. She wasn't the best looking girl in the house nor did she have the best body. She loved what she did and treated every customer as if he was her man. Not to mention she could ride a twelve-inch cock like a cowgirl and took it in her ass like a stone cold freak. She was only allowed to do hand jobs and stimulated sex per house rules, but she always broke the rules and her customers worshipped her for the fringe benefits she bestowed on them. She would clear three thousand in two hours off of her private shows.

She had on her Dominatrix ensemble, a black latex bra with her nipples peaking, through the cutouts and a matching latex garter with the entire front section exposed to reveal her neatly waxed pussy. "Damn, Anjel you got my dick harder than a bag of quarters. Right now you look good as fuck in that get up"

"Thank you 'sweetie I miss you, babe," she drawled as she mounted his lap and started grinding his erect bulge that throbbed thru his denim jeans. "Damn boo from the size of things you missed me too," she chuckled and wrapped her arms around his neck, while he pulled her close and smacked her bare ass cheeks. "Oooh I've been a naughty girl, I'm sorry." Anjel giggled. The customer laughed at her role-playing and slipped a hundred in her garter. He loved how she made him feel like he was the only man she wanted to be with. His night would be fun as long as he didn't run out of money. He knew from past experiences that Anjel would turn ice cold and her juicy vagina that he loved to finger would dry up as soon as the money ran out.

It was the end of a long night, the club was still packed and Anjel's set was over. She was exhausted as she sat in the dressing room smoking a cigarette. "Anjel what are you getting into? wanna go to the waffle house? I'm starving." asked Kitty. She was a Mexican beauty and also an exotic dancer, she favored the actress Selma Hayek, her hair was jet black and curly and it flowed down her back hitting the top of her ass crack. Her thick arched black eyebrows framed her smoldering black eyes that she used to mesmerize men. Kitty's skin was honey colored and she had sexy red ruby lips that she used to tease the men that watched her lick her tongue over them. Kitty was a Latin bombshell, her voluptuous body thick thighs and tiny waist drove men wild. She made a fortune dancing and was Magic City's premier dancer. She made the most money and was very popular. The only problem was, unlike Anjel she despised dancing. Her dream was to become a professional singer. She had a marvelous voice and had the look. J-Lo didn't have shit on Kitty and she knew it.

"OK, girl, lemme call Daisy and see if she wanna meet us there," said Anjel.

"Where Daisy been at?" asked Kitty curiously "I haven't seen her in a minute."

"Girl, my beech hit the jackpot. She got wit' that boy Young Chio" bragged Anjel. She was proud of her best friend's newest conquest.

"No shittin', not Young Chio the millionaire," gasped Kitty in awe.

"Yes, girl, you didn't see his video for Tata Bounce. Daisy is his wifey in the video. She even had a love scene with him. She snatched him up right from the shoot. Bitches were hatin' on my girl but she did the damn thing," laughed Anjel as she and Kitty smacked high-five over Daisy's victory.

Kitty was pissed on the low. She knew if she was in that video shoot, she would have caught Chio's eye before that puta, Daisy. She was jealous of all the attention Daisy received and didn't feel like she deserved it. All the girls at Magic City knew Daisy and either hated her or tolerated her because of Anjel.

Anjel didn't take any crap—she was younger than all of the girls and they didn't know it but she was wild and could beat fire out of any one of their asses. She didn't allow anyone to disrespect her best friend. The girls resented Daisy because of her holier than thou attitude concerning sex. She constantly bragged about being a virgin and how she still got paid without fucking or stripping for a man. All the girls wanted to be like her but most of the dancers were too caught up in the sordid world of selling sex, whether it be a fantasy or pussy. They had lost all innocence and Daisy Jones irritated them.

Anjel and Kitty jumped in Anjel's Benz truck and sped off to meet Daisy at the new twenty-four-hour diner located in the chic Buck Head area of Atlanta. It was the newest hot spot and it was jam-packed with Atlanta's finest. Daisy and Chio were there waiting for them. They had just left Chio's club.

"Girl, Daisy said everybody that's anybody is at 24/7's," Anjel reported excitedly as she clicked off the phone.

"Who's with Chio? I hope one of his fine ass friends especially Geechi," said Kitty, hoping to bump into Geechi. He was a drug kingpin almost as rich if not richer than Chio. His entire crew was handsome. They called themselves the Black Colombian Cartel or BCC for short. They usually hung out with Chio so with any luck the girls would be dining with hunks. The 24/7 entrance was packed when Anjel pulled into the parking lot. She scanned the crowded lot and smiled. She was satisfied with the turnout. The lot resembled a car show—there were Mercedes, Range Rover's, and a few Bentley's sprinkled in for fun. She parked next to a silver Hummer, the size of a small building. The monster truck sat on 40"chrome spinners. Kitty jumped out and stuck her stilleto in between the stokes and playfully nudged the spinning rims "Anjel, it's so much paper in this motherfucker I can smell it. I'm leaving here with a billion dollar Papi tonight," Kitty whooped.

"Holla girl I can't wait to get inside. 'Sheet this place hotter than the damn club, why da hell we had to work tonight we should have been partying with Daisy. You know we would have been all up in V.I.P with Chio and them," said Anjel. She forgot how tired she was from dancing all night, lucky she didn't do the champagne room or she would have been wiped out.

Kitty was roaring to go. She was twenty-four-years-old and had the stamina of a twelve-year-old. She could care less that it was 4:00 am and she had been dancing since 10:00 p.m. The girls had changed into their street clothes which still oozed sex appeal. They sauntered into the restaurant in tiny miniskirts and tiny T-shirts with their tightly toned calves and thighs, they had bodies of athletes with the wanton sex appeal that only exotic dancers offered. Daisy looked up the moment the girls entered the crowded eatery and smiled from ear to ear when she saw how her girls were representing. With, the exception of herself, the girls where the hottest chicks in the spot.

"There they go boo, my girls are here," she nudged Chio so he could have the hostess escort them over to where they were seated. The private section of the diner reserved for celebrities was off in the back of the diner and Daisy loved the vibe in the restaurant. It was classic Hotlanta. All the fab people in Chocolate City were getting their grub on.

Atlanta, GA had it going on because black folks ran shit. Mostly all the public officials, including the mayor, was African American, and the majority of the population were well off. She loved the Buck Head area in Atlanta, that section of the city held many upscale eateries and the diner didn't disappoint. The décor` was impeccable and the cuisine was mouthwatering. They made the best steak and eggs she had ever tasted and the hash browns melted in her mouth. She was happy and content as she ate the delicious food, she had been with Young Chio for two months and they were inseparable. After their trip to Vegas, he asked her to move into his mansion. She couldn't turn him down he gave her fifteen thousand dollars to give her mom to help out with the bills in her absence, now that was some fly shit—she was impressed.

She decided to be straight up with him so she told him her age. To her amazement he loved it. He was twenty-eight but his industry age was eighteen, so having a young girlfriend didn't hurt his image at all. He had millions of lil' girls fawning all over him. Daisy was starting to really feel Chio and that scared her because once she gave him her heart she would start slipping. She had to keep the words of wisdom her mama instilled in her, "Nigga's ain't shit in general and as soon as you start slipping and falling for that love mess that's when he'll use your emotions against you and you will end up laying around having babies tryna keep his sorry ass or start believing the bullshit game he'll start running on you while he out there sticking his thang in every hole he can get it in." Mama Jones would dispense her wisdom on Daisy at a very young age because she knew her beautiful daughter needed to be schooled quickly or she would fall prey to any no good man who pounced on her.

So Daisy knew better than to fall in love but Chio was doing all the right things and his head game was the bomb. He never pressured her for sex and was very satisfied with licking her cat. He was insatiable he would service her in all types of positions. The best was when he picked her up and sat her on his shoulders, then, he stuck his face in her cat and ate her out while he carried her around his indoor pool house. It drove her bonkers as soon as she began to climax he would lower her down and ease her into his Jacuzzi, positioning her cat directly on the powerful jets. Daisy would explode in ecstasy as soon as the warm water hit her clit. She had never experienced an orgasm like that in her life. He blew her mind and she was falling hard for him, but she was determined not to let him know—she wanted to keep the upper hand. There was no doubt in her mind that he was feeling her because he showed her in so many ways, but she still had to keep her guards up because one never knew when a man was going to flip. It was such an uncomfortable feeling because she never gave two shits about a man before. She knew one thing—she wanted him bad and if he continued giving her the royal treatment he was definitely going to get her precious goldmine.

She figured he would be proposing to her soon if he wanted her bad enough. She loved his crazy ass, but he had to wife her before she gave herself to him. "Hey girl what's up?" Anjel greeted Daisy with a warm hug. "Hi Chio," gushed Anjel. She was used to being around ballers, but something about Chio still made her blush he was so damn famous.

"Hey, baby girl, have a seat," he replied. He was in his usual exuberant mood. He had a good night at his club, Jungle. It was 'the' spot to party in Atl and all his people came out to support him. Even a few of the East Coast rappers came through. Dipset's C.E.O Jim Jones was in the building with his boys which brought the already high attendance of ladies to damn near fire hazard status. The place was packed, bottles of *Ciroc* and *Nuvo* flowed all night.

Weezy and *Drake* from *Young Money* stopped in to show him love and introduced him to the newest member of Lil' Wayne's group, Nikki Minaj. She was very sexy and Chio wanted to flirt with her all night but Daisy wasn't having it. All in all, it was a very good night plus he had the baddest bitch by his side Daisy, and she was a stunner. Everybody wanted her and she was all his. The night was young and getting better now that her sexy friends showed up.

Damn, these hoe's got it going on, thought Chio. He couldn't help slyly eyeing Kitty from head to toe. He always had an infatuation for Spanish girls. His dick was getting hard just thinking about slaying that Latin P-bone. "Hey Daisy," Kitty greeted her with a wide smile. She was happy for the opportunity to slide Chio her number the first chance she got. She had a sex radar that was flashing bright lights and felt Chio lusting over her. She had no loyalty to Daisy. *Fuck that puta,* Kitty thought. *I'm going to steal her man right from under her nose.*

"Hola, Chio. ¿Cómo estás?" she said, giggling as she flirted with Chio in Spanish.

She knew her sexy accent would turn him on. Daisy looked at Kitty and smiled wickedly. She peeped the flirting and although she didn't like it she allowed it. She wanted to see how Chio handled himself, plus she was used to women throwing themselves at her man—after all, he was a superstar. She didn't expect much from Kitty, she knew she was envious of her, yet she kept her close. Mama Jones always told her "Keep your enemies close, especially if she a hoe." So Daisy let Kitty play herself. "What up, Mami. Have a seat. My boo told me she had some bad ass friends and she wasn't lying why y'all ain't come to the jungle tonight?"

Anjel answered before Kitty could continue disrespecting her friend "We had to work and besides that Daisy didn't call to remind me. Her damn fingers broke since you done kidnapped her ass," pouted Anjel playfully as she winked at Daisy.

That's my beech, Daisy thought. She was pleased that Anjel made that comment. She wanted Chio to know she gave him all her attention. "That's right," Chio said. "My baby can't leave my side. She gotta take care of her Daddy," he said, throwing his arm around Daisy. He damn near blinded Anjel and Kitty with his diamond flooded Jacob the Jeweler watch.

Kitty had been with many rich men but never had she seen one sporting such flawless diamonds with stones as big as pebbles. 'This guy is the truth.' She couldn't control herself as she rubbed her leg up against his under the table, her lust for Chio made her bold. She knew that once he heard her voice and felt her legs wrapped around him with her special vise grip she used to seduce and control in bed she would have him. "Chio did Daisy tell you I am a singer?" Kitty purred, knowing she was completely playing herself. The worst thing you could do with an entertainer is to bring up trying to get into the game. It was so tacky and besides the fact that if Daisy wanted Chio to know about Kitty's aspiring singing career she would have told him herself.

"Actually" Daisy interrupted, "I never mentioned it, but if you want to drop your demo off, I will see that he gets it," she smirked and gave Kitty a smug smile as to say don't hold your breath bitch.

"Whatever my boo says." Chio felt the tension brewing and decided to agree with Daisy to avoid the drama. He really wanted to drop her off so he could screw the hell out of her friend. *Damn*, he thought. *I could rip shawty right now. She's a bold lil' freak.* He knew what time it was as soon as he felt her rub against his leg. He had to figure out a way to get her digits. Kitty was one step ahead of him.

"Oh, I got my CD right on me." She dug in her Hermes bag and handed her CD to Chio, smiling innocently at Daisy. Chio grinned and stuck the CD in his pocket.

"I'll listen to it later, Shawty, and see what you're working wit." He knew her contact info would be on her CD and thanked God for wannabe singers. He slept with most of them from Mississippi to Atlanta. They traveled near and far to become stars.

Everybody wanted to shine but not very many had the actual talent to back it up, but what they lacked in talent they made up for it in the bedroom. "Oh, shit. My nigga, Anthony Davis is in this motherfucker," shouted Chio.

Daisy panicked as she spun around and spotted the ball player as he walked in the diner with his entourage. She could have crawled under the table at that moment. She had no idea Chio and Anthony was cool and knew she had to disappear or all hell would break loose.

"Anjel come with me to the bathroom." Daisy kicked Anjel under the table so she would catch on that they had to make a speedy exit. Anjel was already telling Kitty to come on she tried to pull her out of her seat.

"I don't have to pee," whined Kitty.

Daisy glared at her in disgust and signaled to Anjel to let her stay. She didn't want Anthony to see her and kick dirt on her to Chio, so the girls made a hasty retreat to the bathroom. Seconds later Anthony Davis was headed to the V.I.P section of the diner to be seated.

"Shit," muttered Daisy, "we gotta get the hell outta here, Anjel. I don't want that fool to see me."

"I know, D, that dumb beech Kitty playing games. I tol' her ass to come on," Anjel spat, pissed off and feeling guilty because she realized Kitty was trying to fuck Chio and she was responsible for bringing the snake around.

"That beech thinks she slick," Daisy said. "I'll catch up with her ass later. Let me text Chio and tell him I'll catch up with him later."

"Huh? How you gonna leave like that?" Anjel questioned Daisy's hasty move. She didn't wanna leave yet the diner was poppin'.

"Girl, if Anthony sees me he's gonna hate and I don't need him telling my baby no bullshit, so we're gonna act like you had an accident and messed up your skirt, you know, like your period came." Daisy paced the marble bathroom floors concocting a plausible story.

"Why I have to be the one bleeding all over myself, it will be better if you say it was you." Anjel rationalized. "You're right," agreed Daisy as she typed Chio a message on her pink jewel encrusted iPhone. "I told him to drop that whore Kitty off," said Daisy. Anjel looked at Daisy like she had two heads.

"Are you nuts? You see how that tramp is all over him."

"I'm no fool Miss Honey," Daisy said, imitating her transsexual hairstylist, Labasia. He talked shit all day in his exaggerated feminine voice.

Anjel burst out laughing "Girl, you know you a fool."

"No, darling. Miss Hoe Cake is the fool if she thinks she can play me. I'm letting her dig a hole so I can bury her trifling ass in it. Plus, I will see if Chio loves me enough to keep his dick still." With that Daisy spun around in her thousand dollars stilettos, swinging her matching purse in a dramatic fashion, sashaying toward the exit. Anjel followed her, cracking up with laughter.

CHAPTER 4

Chio had just finished reading his message from Daisy explaining her hasty departure when Anthony Davis stopped by to greet him. "Yo, man, I didn't know you was in town. I woulda threw you a party at my spot," said Chio graciously. He loved throwing lavish parties and used every opportunity to party.

Anthony Davis was a popular baller. Like Allen Iverson, he was the league's bad boy on and off the court. Chio knew all the A-list ballplayers in the industry. Everybody who was anybody wanted to be a friend of young Chio's. He was one of the few high profile players in the music industry that was on the top of his game and still a down to earth guy. He never beefed with any other rappers and was well known for his smash parties and his generosity. If he was in a magnanimous mood he would open his bar and share his best bottles of champagne and liquor for free. He coined the term buying-the-bar-out. He loved to have a good time, was filthy rich and could afford the extravagance.

"I didn't even know I was heading this way. I have to take care of some unfinished business," replied Anthony. He hadn't been in Atlanta since his break up with Daisy. He was traded to the New York Knicks, but he injured his knee and wanted to do his intense physical therapy in Atlanta on his offseason. Ultimately he wanted to see Daisy again. He couldn't get the gold digging witch out of his system. She had put a spell on him that he tried to snap out of, but was proving very difficult. He didn't know what he wanted to do to her. It was a cross between screwing her until she bled to death or choking the shit out of her. That little bitch deserved to be taught a lesson. Anthony planned to be her teacher.

"Aight, Ant, holla at ya dude when you free up and come thru the jungle let me know beforehand so I can set you up a nice private section of the club with some of my wildcats," offered Chio.

"That's what's up pimpin'. I heard about those bad ass females you keep in the jungle." Anthony grinned and gestured towards Kitty who basked in the compliment and loved the attention she received from the two stars. Anthony gave Chio a pound and left to be seated with his boys.

Chio looked at Kitty and his hard-on returned he couldn't believe his good fortune. Daisy had to leave suddenly leaving him alone with the stunning beauty. Frankly, he could care less where Daisy had to go. He wanted Kitty and the party had just begun. "So, Mami what you wanna get into? ya girls left you, Daisy had to take care of something," Chio said giving Kitty a knowing smile. Kitty licked her luscious lips and pulled out her Mac glass lip gloss and applied the thick gooey gloss to her lips slowly enticing Chio with the erotic show.

"Let's hang out Papi I got some X. Wanna roll wit' me?" she purred, offering him the popular drug ecstasy.

She sold X and cocaine, supplying the strippers who indulged at the club. Some of them couldn't perform without the drug. It served as an aphrodisiac for them. Kitty had a profitable business going it paid for her studio sessions and kept up her lavish lifestyle along with the money she made dancing. She was also addicted to the powerful pills. She loved how they made her feel. She could fuck for hours on a single pill. She had pure MDNA, straight up X, no mix. She called her pills "good pussy." Like good sex her brand had her customers whipped.

"Shawty, what you rollin' wit' I only swallow good pussy," replied Chio referring to the brand of pills she sold.

"That's my shit Papi," said Kitty. She was excited that he used her brand. She pulled out a Tylenol bottle filled with singles doubles and triple stacks.

"Get the fuck outta here. You must cop from my boy Poncho out in College Park he just hit me off with a suitcase full of that shit. I fill up my candy dishes in the Jungle with that good ole pussy," said Chio hyped up at the prospect of fucking Kitty with some ecstasy dick. He could screw for hours on end without having an orgasm. All he needed was water, orange juice and plenty of KY Jelly for the P-bone he was putting it down on cuz he was sure to dry it up. He couldn't wait to hit Daisy off. She would regret making him wait. "Gimme a triple stack, Mami, I'm ready," he instructed her.

"Here Papi" Kitty slipped the powerful pill inside of his mouth and joined him with a pill of her own. They washed the pills down with water and anticipated the euphoric effects of the drugs.

An hour later Chio was sitting on Kitty's bed looking at the top of her head bob up and down as she sucked him dry. He stroked her curly hair admiring her exotic beauty. He loved strippers and hadn't been to Magic's in a minute. Since meeting Daisy at his Video shoot he had been too occupied trying to get into her panties. He loved the challenge, but he also missed his freak sessions with the professional sexperts like Kitty. It was nothing like a wild night with a nympho. "Awww, Mami, damn. take your tongue out my ass girl that shit feel funny." Chio squirmed, feeling feminine but he couldn't help his dick from getting hard as a brick as soon as her tongue grazed his butt. "Just lick my nuts don't mess wit' my asshole," demanded Chio. *This nasty bitch tryna turn a nigga out*, he thought. "Turn over," he commanded.

Kitty spun around on her knees and cocked her legs up on the bed. She was in the pushup position with Chio in between her legs, she was ready to get her freak on—her pussy was twitchin', throbbing. Her cunt was steaming. The X had taken effect and she wanted to be thoroughly fucked. She had butterflies in her stomach from the anticipation.

"Papi, please fuck me in my bootie and use this for my *chocha*," she pleaded, handing him a ten-inch chocolate-colored vibrator from under her bed.

Chio laughed hysterically "Holy shit, Mami. You want to freak off in this motherfucker, huh? No problem Papi sure will take care of ya fresh ass." He took the vibrator from her and held it next to his penis. "Shit how many inches is this?"

"Ten inches," answered Kitty, admiring her love toy.

"Well look here your boy is two inches longer than your lil' friend here, how 'bout that." Chio grinned like a hyena, proud of his huge cock. It swelled so long and thick it resembled a mini bat. He hunched over Kitty's voluptuous ass and slid his iron-hard rod inside of her dripping wet vagina. "Ugg," he grunted in satisfaction. She sucked him inside of her like she was a vacuum. He leaned back so he could get the vibrator in her ass without ripping her or causing her pain. The length of his penis prevented him from slipping out. He never skipped a stroke. He had the vibrator in sync with the strokes he pumped her with.

"Ooooh—Ahh, it feels so damn good Papi," Kitty moaned in pure bliss. It felt like heaven to her. She didn't even mind that Chio didn't use the vibrator in her pussy like she wanted him to. He did justice with his penis. She was kind of nervous with him going in her anus with the toy but he handled her with care surprisingly enough. He proved to be an expert with the toy.

She felt her vagina muscles contracting and her anus relaxing as he stuck the toy further inside of her. He rotated and thrust all in the same motion. They went at it for an hour until she finally fought the effects of the drug and climaxed from both holes.

Chio was in his glory. He felt like a beast slaying his willing prey. He beat his fist against his chest, and roared, "I'm king cock."

"Yes, yes, Papi. You are my king cock," Kitty yelled. She jumped up, reenergized at the thought of his fat iron rod throbbing inside of her. He came all over her body when he pulled out, spraying her with his passion and marking her with his scent. She pranced around her king-size canopy bed and twirled her legs around the bedpost. "King put my CD on so I can perform for you, baby," purred Kitty swaying seductively to an imaginary beat. The dried cum on her belly and nipples drove Chio nuts.

"Fuck that CD, Mami. Sing to me while you sit on my dick," he demanded bluntly. He didn't have to ask her twice. Kitty was ready for round two, her juices were flowing like a rainforest. Normally, she would have been too sore and dry to even think about another round, but she turned into Wonder Woman when she was on X. She tried to fuck Chio's dreads loose. She climbed on top of him and grind his dick to the melody in her head while serenading Chio with her beautiful song.

Chio was in heaven. He pumped her drenched p-bone slow and deep while she sang the sexiest song he had ever heard. Her voice was pure and angelic, a mix between Keyshia Cole, and the late Aaliyah. He knew as he thrust deeper and deeper, matching her grind for grind, she was going to be a star. Everything about her was right—the voice, the face, her body, even her p-bone was platinum status. He beat her pussy for another hour while he mentally made plans to record her and make her the first lady of his label.

* * *

"Where is this nigga at?" exploded Daisy as she paced back and forth in Anjel's living room.

"That nasty hoe Kitty ain't picking up her phone, either," Anjel informed Daisy after dialing Kitty's phone for the fourth time.

"I know they are somewhere laid up fucking. He ain't stupid enough to bring her home so they're either laid up in a 'telly or at that slut's house," Daisy deduced, plotting her revenge. "OK, let's face facts. I'm not sleeping with Chio, so he's getting his rocks off with that slut bucket. Cool, no problem. He played himself by sticking it in a bitch that I'm supposed to be cool with. That bastard is going to pay for that," declared Daisy. She sank down into Anjel's couch and closed her eyes. Her head was pounding and she screamed in anguish from the agony of betrayal. She was so angry that she could have killed Young Chio and the stank hoe Kitty. "Nigga's ain't shit, especially rich ones. He probably doesn't even think he's doing anything wrong. Stupid motherfucker." Anjel sat quietly beside her best friend, allowing her to vent. She felt her pain, she knew it was best to let her get all her frustration out and prayed she didn't turn on her for bringing Kitty around. Anjel loved Daisy and couldn't stand when she was mad at her. Throughout their friendship, they never had one fight, mainly because Anjel let Daisy call the shots, not because she feared her, but more so out of respect. Daisy was the only family she had after her mother died and had it not been for her love and support she would not have made it through the foster homes, especially the last one.

The family she had been placed with were savages and Daisy helped her escape. The father, Mr. Johnson, tried to molest Anjel while she showered. When she fought him off and told his wife, she flipped out on Anjel and beat her with a cast iron pan. She told Daisy; and, her best friend came through for her. She wired Anjel some money for a bus ticket out of that hell hole and she never looked back. Fuck foster care. Anjel decided she could take care of herself just fine without being beaten or raped. Daisy hooked her up with the owner of Magic City Strip Club and the rest was history. Anjel had found her calling. She lied about her age, used a fake ID, and at fourteen she became an exotic dancer. She loved it. She didn't understand why Daisy didn't want to work there, but she respected her hustle. Gold digging without giving up the booty was gangster. Daisy was her hero. She could never have pulled that one off. She loved sex far too much to hold on to her virginity. She glanced at Daisy and slid her arm around her shoulder pulling her in for a hug. "D, you'll be alright you will do what you do best—make that bastard pay."

"I gotta be real with you Anjel, I was starting to fall for the asshole, I'm glad this happened it put me back on my A game." Daisy jumped off the couch suddenly, and shouted, "I'm back, bitch. Daisy Jones is back. No more of that mushy mama shit," she said, quoting a line from her favorite rapper. "I got an idea, let's get some rest. I'm staying here for a few days so that nigga can feel it. Let's see how he feels after we go shopping on him, guess what I did?" Daisy asked Anjel with a devilish smirk on her face.

"Uh uh, what you done did beech?" giggled Anjel.

"I got that dog's unlimited black American Express card. He let me hold it last week and forgot to get it back," she stated triumphantly. "We're going to Chanel tomorrow."

"I know that's right, D." Anjel and Daisy hi-fived and headed off to shower and get ready for bed.

Anjel lived in a plush townhouse on Peach Street down the road from the Lennox Mall. They were walking distance to the finest upscale shops in Atlanta. They planned to have a ball the next day.

Anjel got out of the shower and rubbed body oil on her body while Daisy smoked a blunt to relieve her migraine. Anjel had scented candles placed throughout her crib and the aroma had a calming effect on Daisy. Anjel glanced at her and noticed Daisy staring at her with glazed lustful eyes as she rubbed lotion on her body. Anjel immediately became aroused she couldn't stop her nipples from hardening and the sudden moistness between her legs was an indication that Anjel wanted Daisy. They had done *it* once before around the time Anjel discovered her mom was dying. They innocently found comfort in each other's arms and one thing led to another. Anjel was distraught and Daisy kissed her, the loving gesture turned into a passionate embrace that either one of them repeated or mentioned. Anjel knew what was happening and allowed the moment to take place. She walked over to Daisy and slipped her arms around her naked body, her friend needed comfort and Anjel was going to do her best to make her forget her heartache at least for the night.

Daisy inhaled the blunt she was smoking and gave Anjel a kiss while she blew the strong marijuana deep into Anjel's throat. As Anjel inhaled the potent smoke she took Daisy's hand and led her to the bed. Neither girl spoke a word. Daisy laid on her back and pulled Anjel gently on top of her. They held each other as their bodies glided together smoothly. The silkiness of the body oil allowed them to form one sexy body of entwined breast hips and legs with ease. Daisy gasped with pleasure when she felt the heat from Anjel's juicy love box rub against her own, their clits stuck together like magnets and found a rhythm. She spread her legs and formed a scissor position allowing Anjel to feel her cat and grind against her passionately. They kissed gently at first, soft tongue against soft tongue, little feathery licks exploring each other's wet mouths until their excitement built and they needed more. Daisy grabbed Anjel's face and stuck her tongue deep in her mouth, Anjel sucked her tongue tasting her sweet breath mixed with the weed she had been smoking. Both aromas turned her on. She kissed her neck and breast licking her nipples like a kitten lapping hungrily at its milk bowl. She felt Daisy's nipples harden until they felt like marbles in her mouth. She sucked them harder. Daisy widened her legs and bucked her body wildly against Anjel's wanting more. Anjel licked a path down towards Daisy's precious goldmine. Her vagina was bald and smooth, she licked her entire vagina starting on the fatty front then she parted her lips and lapped up the juices that glistened on Daisy's clit. She slid her tongue deep until she entered her womanhood and stuck her face where she knew was untouched and pure. She felt Daisy's muscles contract and squeezed her tongue. She became so turned on by the idea of tongue fucking her best friend that she felt herself climaxing as she slammed her tongue in and out of Daisy's pussy in a wild frenzy.

Daisy grind her face until she felt herself explode the girls came simultaneously. They were both panting for air and feeling the aftermath of electric sparks pulsating through their bodies. They were sated. The orgasm satisfied their heat and sealed their bond. If nothing else they had each other, best friends with benefits. Daisy smiled at Anjel and they fell into a blissful sleep. Their bodies entwined tightly, both dreaming about the shopping spree and how much they loved each other.

CHAPTER 5

It was Saturday afternoon and the Lennox Mall was packed. Daisy still hadn't heard from Chio she refused to call him again. If he wanted her he would have to find her. She had some major shopping to do at his expense. They pulled up in front of valet parking in front of the mall entrance and stepped out of Daisy's Beemer. The sexy girls looked like celebrities walking on the red carpet. Anjel loved the attention she received when she rolled with Daisy. She was pretty, but Daisy had an aura about her that made people stop and take notice. Daisy Jones had star appeal and she knew it. The valet line could pass for a night club's parking lot. Lennox Mall was a social gathering for Atlanta's elite. A stretch Hummer pulled up behind them and out popped five of the sexy burlesque dancers from the girl group *The Pussy Cat Dolls*. Daisy noticed Nicole the leader of the group was absent. She loved the song, *Stick With You,* and wanted to give Nicole props on her vocals.

The Lennox Mall was the most exciting upscale mall in Atlanta and Daisy's favorite place to shop. "Girl, let's go directly to Chanel. You know I love her," said Daisy with exaggerated goo-goo eyes.

"Come on silly gal, let's go spend your man's money." Anjel pulled her to their first stop, the ever fabulous Chanel boutique. They felt the luxuriant ambiance as soon as they stepped on the plush monogrammed carpet of the store. Daisy's favorite salesperson rushed to her side as soon as he spotted her. "Good Afternoon Ms. Jones. It's wonderful to see you today. You are looking ravishing as usual," gushed Antonio happily. He greeted her with the reverence reserved for all of his big spenders. He knew she wasn't going to waste his time browsing. She always spent at least three-grand with him. He drooled over her as he mentally calculated the commission from his sales.

"Thanks, Antonio. I'd like to check out the new line of bags and bring out that coat I tried on last time."

"Darlin, that was a magnificent selection and I see the piece was calling you." He clapped his hands with glee. Last time she shopped there she had admired the $15,000 exclusive chinchilla lined denim jacket. Antonio could have jumped for joy. He knew he was going to have a good day. He told his boyfriend that morning before he left for work that he felt money coming because his hand wouldn't stop itching. His lover joked that he could stop the itching by stroking the hard-on he had for him. Antonio smiled widely at the memory of the lovemaking that followed and now he was about to see the money that he felt coming. Ms. Daisy was going to make him a pretty piece of change. "Yes, Darlin', I shall bring out the fabulous creation—it's got your name written all over it," he said as he glided off to retrieve the expensive piece.

"As a matter of fact, bring one for my friend, too." Daisy smiled lovingly at Anjel, who squealed with excitement and hugged her. Antonio had to stop himself from hugging Daisy as well.

"Thanks, girl," gushed Anjel.

"No problem. You deserve it boo—you always have my back." Daisy had a flash-back of the erotic night they spent together and was ready to spend all Chio's money on her best friend for the bomb head she gave her. Daisy proceeded to rack up 50,000 dollars worth of fly utterly expensive Chanel wear.

Two hours later they were dining on seafood in the food court surrounded by Chanel bags making themselves the envy of every shopper that passed by. Having that many packages from the notably expensive store signified that the girls were working with some major paper and seeing females doing their thing like that was admirable. "Oooh Daisy, when Chio gets a whiff of his bill he is going to flip out," giggled Anjel a bit nervously.

"Fuck that asshole," Daisy said in disgust "He must still be fucking that whore. He hasn't called me yet," Daisy seethed. "Humph." She sucked her teeth. "I'm not finished with his ass yet. As soon as we're done eating we're going to Jeffrey's to cop us those Jacob the Jeweler crocodile sneakers I want."

"Daisy those tennis shoes cost $7,500 a-piece," said Anjel.

"And? We are getting them," Daisy replied coolly.

"OK, with me. It's just his card might decline," Anjel whispered uneasily.

"Girl, this is his *unlimited* Black Amex—we can buy a house with this, baby."

"I know that's right." Anjel slapped Daisy five and finished cracking her lobster tail.

"Hey girl," Daisy waived at the sales girl Gina as they entered the chic trendy boutique, Jeffrey's. "I want to order two pairs of Jacob croc sneakers with the 2.5-carat diamond bezels encrusted in them," She said casually.

"Huh." Gina was flabbergasted. She knew Daisy was a shopaholic from her past spending sprees, but $15,000 for two pairs of sneakers was an unusual purchase.

"How are you paying?" the woman asked, eyeing Daisy suspiciously. She wasn't trying to lose her job over no fraud shit.

"Excuse me?" Daisy's eyebrows shot up and she gave the cashier a look of disdain as if the girl farted. "What did you ask me?"

"I asked you how were you paying—cash or charge," asked Gina, refusing to back down or be intimidated by Daisy.

Meanwhile, Daisy was pissed and highly offended by her attitude, but she kept her cool, determined to spend Chio's money without the disturbance of this insolent bitch. She knew she had to convince the girl to trust her or scare her into processing the transaction without suspicion.

"I'm paying how I usually pay—in full." Daisy took a thick wad of hundred dollar bills out of her wallet and pretended to count. She pretended to yawn, and said, "Matter fact, Anjel, I should use my black card and hold on to my cash for the club tonight."

"Yeah, girl, you know we gonna get our drink on and I want to start off with two bottles of Ciroc," Anjel said, playing along with Daisy's game. Gina felt stupid for suspecting Daisy of foul play and hurried to the counter to ring her up.

Anjel glanced at Daisy and they burst out laughing. "Silly pig. What did she think? You were gonna give her a stolen credit card?" Anjel chuckled.

"Shit, I wish his bitch ass would report this card stolen. I'll kill his disrespectful ass," Daisy swore angrily, getting heated all over again as she thought about his betrayal.

"I ordered the tennis shoes and they will be shipped to your house in two days Ms. Jones" Gina stated humbly.

"You don't have any in stock?" Daisy asked irritated by the delay.

"They are so exclusive we only take orders for them," explained Gina apologetically. She was a rather plain looking heavyset white girl and she dreamed of looking as good as the girls she waited on. She was green with envy. *These niggers don't deserve to live like this*, she thought.

"Will that be all you need today?" she managed to produce a fake smile.

"Actually," Daisy smirked, "you can give me two pair of those *Christian Dior* shades over there." She pointed to the glass showcase filled with different brands of designer shades. As Anjel tried on the CD shades with the rhinestones blinging around the lens Daisy noticed two females creeping sneakily into the store. She smiled as she recognized the girls. She did business with them all the time. They were boosters. Thieves.

The twin sisters Coco and Casey were originally from New York. They made a killing stealing high-end merchandise and selling the gear for half price around the city. Daisy knew what they were up to so she nudged Anjel and nodded her head in the girls' direction. Anjel knew what time it was as soon as she recognized the popular thieves and like Daisy she wasn't going to blow up the twins' spot. They kept the cashier occupied by trying on several pairs of shades until they saw the twins wobble out of the store, their girdles loaded with merchandise. Daisy marveled at how boosters hid everything in between their legs by stuffing the items in the body girdles they wore it was amazing. As the twins exited the store Gina glanced at them totally clueless that the girls robbed her blind. *That will teach this bitch about watching the wrong people,* Daisy thought, chuckling to herself.

She glanced at Anjel and gave her a knowing smile. Anjel giggled and rolled her eyes at the dumb salesgirl. Bored with browsing, Daisy picked out a pair of cute shades for herself and the CD shades for Anjel. "OK, this should do it," she told Gina and handed her the credit card.

DAISY JONES

"Um, Ms. Jones, this card doesn't have your name on it," Gina challenged Daisy, happy to have the upper hand again.

"Sweetie, let me explain something to you. This is a company card issued to the C.E.O of the company which you see the card has the name of a very prominent Record Label of which I am the vice president. American Express issues this particular type of card to their privileged members. It is the *unlimited* Black Edition and if there is a problem with me using my card here I will simply take my business elsewhere," Daisy stated, glaring at the cashier with a look that could have melted ice.

"No problem, Ms. Jones." Gina slid the card and completed the transaction. She decided it wasn't wise to keep going back and forth with Daisy. If her manager got a whiff of her losing a twenty thousand dollar sale she would be fired immediately.

Anjel admired Daisy's game. She had the poise and vocabulary of an educated corporate woman. It always amazed Anjel when she witnessed Daisy performing. She could have won an Academy Award for best acting. It was hard to believe she was so young. They both grew up fast, but Daisy was light years ahead of her as far as intellect. She was very mature. Anjel's mom always said Daisy had an old soul. That was one of the reasons that Anjel let Daisy lead—she was more than qualified.

When the girls left the store they shared a hearty laugh and recapped the scene in the store. When they spotted the twins again they were walking fast towards the mall's exit. "Hey twins,

61

what's up—y'all got something for us?" Anjel called after the girls.

"Yeah ma but we gotta get up outta here. We will holla at y'all later and good lookin' for keeping home girl busy in Jeffrey's," Coco thanked them and kept it moving.

Anjel knew it was Coco because of the scar on her face. The battle mark gave her a rough edge but made it easy to distinguish her from her sister.

"No sweat honey, you know how we do. Meet us at the salon and don't let Labasia buy all the good stuff," Daisy chirped in referring to their hair stylist at their favorite salon. The twins made a lot of money at the salon. It was one of the central meeting spots to knock off their wares. In a blink of an eye, the twins had disappeared out of the mall. They were gone in a New York minute, moving fast like most city folks do. "Damn those two gals don't play any games," said Anjel.

"Shit ain't nobody more official than us we just spent seventy thousand in three hours," bragged Daisy. As they stepped into Daisy's Beemer she tipped the valet fifty dollars and waited for him to load their bags in the trunk.

"I know that's fucking right, beech," Anjel whooped and slapped her girl a high-five.

"Now that's what I call getting even with a nigga." Daisy clicked on her radio and burst out laughing when Young Chio's song 'Tata bounce' blared through her speakers. Daisy bounced her perky breast to the beat and rolled with laughter as she pulled out of the mall.

CHAPTER 6

Anthony couldn't believe his luck. He had only been in Atlanta 48 hours and had already spotted Daisy. He didn't know how he was going to catch up with her because he never knew where she lived so when he saw two fine shorties with fat asses strut by him loaded down with shopping bags he did a double take. He started to' holla at one of them before he recognized Daisy's unmistakable strut and her thick, pretty, long curly hair. No other chocolate sister in Atlanta had such beautiful natural long hair. He ducked into a store quickly before she noticed him. *I got you now bitch*, he thought excitedly. He had to admit his penis got hard immediately from seeing her fine ass, he obviously wasn't over her.

He followed her as she spent what he assumed was his money. He fumed when he thought about how she played him. The grimy gold-digging bitch even got a BMW from him. She owed him big time. She had crushed his ego and to add insult to injury, he still wanted her. She was all he thought about he was totally obsessed with Daisy. He couldn't get his dick hard when he had sex without thinking about her. It had gotten so bad he confided in his mother she was the only woman on the planet that he trusted, he knew without a doubt she loved him unconditionally.

She was responsible for his success. After his father died of a heart attack she held the family together. She and Anthony moved to Atlanta to live with her parents because she wanted her son to have a decent life. She didn't want him growing up in New York with no father figure. The streets would have eaten Anthony up and she refused to see her baby turn into a statistic like so many other young black boys with no fathers in their life. Bringing Anthony to the south at the tender age of fourteen was the best thing his mother could have ever done. He excelled in the southern school system and became an all-star athlete, he played baseball, football, and basketball and his beloved mother never missed a game. He was the star running back on his football team and the best point guard on his basketball team and went on to become the second overall pick in the NBA Draft. He won the Schick NBA rookie of the year after averaging 25.5 points and 7.5 assists per game. He was a superstar and his mother was the proudest woman on earth. She bragged endlessly about Anthony's achievements. So when he confided in her about Daisy and she saw how depressed he was she went ballistic.

He winced as he recalled how she went off on him calling him a fool for letting a piece of ass effect his game. He knew that if his mother ever found out her age and that he never even had sex with her she would really lose it. Anthony was a mama's boy and longed to please his mother. She advised him to get over the tramp and move on—the problem was it wasn't that simple. The tramp used him and bruised his ego and his pride wouldn't let it go. He didn't want to jeopardize his career but he had to pay Daisy Jones a visit.

He had a hard-on that wouldn't go down as soon as he saw Daisy bouncing her luscious breast to the music in "his" car. He began sweating profusely as he navigated through the heavy traffic on the Buford Highway. It was September and unusually hot even for Atlanta. He turned on the air conditioner in his rented Suburban SUV and followed Daisy as she drove to her destination totally unaware that he was trailing her. Anthony planned to find out where she lived and plot out his course of revenge. He was in deep thought as he listened to Jay-Z's *Empire State of Mind* bobbing his head to the New York anthem. He always 'repped his home state proudly, he was in a zone. He drifted off into a daydream about making love to Daisy "Damn," he roared, shaking his head violently, snapping out of the reverie. *This bitch gotta pay,* he thought. She had him fucked up in the head. He really had plans on making her his wife. Then she had to mess things up with the underage bullshit. She came from left field when she dropped that bomb on him, but he had a trick for her. He was going to claim what was rightfully his regardless of her age or if she wanted it. No one shitted on Anthony Davis like Daisy did and he wasn't going to let her get away with it.

CHAPTER 7

Chio woke up late Sunday evening. He and Kitty were comatose after their Olympic freak off session. They started early Saturday morning and twenty-four hours later they were finally worn out. His penis was aching from his supernatural performance—he literally fucked the shit out of Kitty. The last round he remembered before passing out ended with him wiping feces off his penis. The freak Kitty let loose of her bowels on him, he should have kept screwing her with the vibrator but he wanted to feel the tightness of her ass. *And what the hell was wrong with him?* he thought, questioning himself. He was definitely slipping he remembered going raw dog inside of her. He shook his dreads wildly in disgust while staring lustfully at the sleeping beauty.

She's fine as hell but I hope this hoe ain't sick. Chio cringed at the thought. He hopped out of Kitty's bed, picked his jeans up off the floor, and searched for his blackberry pager. He knew half of Atlanta was trying to reach him. He also knew besides his manager and accountant, Daisy's call was a priority. She was going to kill him. *Damn.* He noticed she had called him a few times Saturday morning after he had left her. He checked his text messages and read one that disturbed him it read "Nigga I hope that nasty pussy was good to you because you'll never taste my goldmine anymore," signed Ms. Jones. OK, she was pissed but she was talking a little too greasy and Chio didn't like it. She didn't have proof that he fucked Kitty and who dat bitch think she talking to,' Chio muttered to himself. He was nice and all but he felt he was too rich to tolerate that type of disrespect from anybody especially a lil' young ass girl that he wasn't even getting any p-bone from. Shit, she should have been grateful that he was waiting around for her stingy ass. He would show Ms. Daisy who called the shots. Shit, this Puerto Rican *mami* what's her name? He racked his brain desperately trying to recall her name, well anyway she was just as bad as Daisy, maybe even 'better, and she could sing like Mariah. Daisy has to understand she can't fuck wit' my money. *Ole girl is fittin' ta make me richer than I already am,* rationalized Chio as he calculated the profits he would receive after her CD went triple platinum.

He glanced at Kitty and admired her voluptuous body as she slept naked on her black silk sheets. His penis started to feel better so he crept over and stroked her silky hair gently. The sunlight crept through the window cashing a golden shadow across her pretty face. He leaned over and nibbled on her neck. Kitty stirred lazily and turned over pulling him on top of her.

"Hola, Papi," she said in a raspy voice. It was hoarse from screaming passionately all night. *"Tu quiero mas chulo?"* Kitty smiled seductively inviting Chio to have some more loving.

"What you said, Mami?"

"Do you want more of me?" she purred, feeling aroused even after the all-nighter they pulled. She thought she was dreaming but her vagina was sore and her booty ached so she knew it was real. She had made wild love to Young Chio all night. She won. Daisy was finito for sure and she knew it. Kitty wrapped her arms around Chio's neck and snuggled close to him. She was so happy that he spent the night with her. She put it on his ass.

"King Cock is ready for more of his *chocha?*" she murmured as she licked his nipples and kissed a trail down his stomach leading to his massive penis. She squeezed it hard and stroked it until Chio growled and commanded she suck it for him. Happily obliging she kissed the mushroom head of his enormous dick and licked the shaft. She let saliva drip from her mouth and lapped the dribble up like he was an ice cream sandwich. She gave Chio a performance worthy of an Oscar and although she didn't like to deep throat, her oral technique was amazing. She focused more on stimulating his sensory nerves on the underside of his penis. She read an article that explained what a man's phallic reacted to when receiving oral sex. Most girls focused on deep throating and didn't give the base of the penis enough attention. Kitty made love to Chio with her mouth, "Right there, Mami," moaned Chio. "Yeah, baby lick it like that, babe." Chio felt so good, he began grinding his cock into her face while she chased his dick with her tongue. He humped her mouth while she kept the pace sucking and licking him softly. *This girl is serious*, Chio thought as his eyes rolled back in his head. Although delirious, he exploded in her face and finally remembered her name. He screamed it loud as he came. "KITTTTTTTTYYY."

CHAPTER 8

Daisy drove directly to Star Status Styles, she and Anjel needed pampering. The girls were completely spent from their arduous shopping spree. Honestly, Daisy was a little nervous. She knew Chio was going to flip out when he discovered she robbed him. She almost called him and told him to report his credit card stolen so he wouldn't be liable for the charges she put on the card. Then she visualized him sucking Kitty like he did her and became furious again, not to mention the cashier at Jeffrey's would love to tell the police who she was. She was too well known in the mall, he would just have to pay the bill and deal with it. It wouldn't hurt his account he was damn near a billionaire. She was confident that he didn't want to lose her over a mere seventy grand. She was worth every cent, she grinned as she parked in the parking lot of the salon. "What are you smiling about?" asked Anjel smiling back at Daisy. She was overjoyed with her gifts from the shopping spree.

"Just thinking about how Chio is gonna flip out when his accountant calls him about the charges," Daisy giggled with glee.

"Girl, I would love to be a fly on the wall when he finds out you went shopping on his ass," Anjel laughed hysterically as they strutted into the salon.

Star Status Styles resembled a mini-mall—it was 6,000 square ft with an adjoining 1,000 square ft parking lot. The building was constructed out of black mirrors. The type of glass that showed your reflection from the outside but obstructed the view of the inside. The salon's name was spelled out in Swarovski crystals on a four-feet marquee. Star Status was the epitome of luxury and high maintenance. The owner was a retired supermodel named Miosha. She employed the elite of the cosmetology industry. Leading the pack was the very fabulous *Labasia*—the transvestite was world renowned for *her* work with hair extensions and lace front wigs. *She* created magic for all the top models and many A-list celebrities who would fly *her* in for occasions when fabulosity was required. Labasia never disappointed and the best part of *her* work was her outrageous personality. The transvestite was hilarious. *She* used to be a drag queen and told *her* clients funny tales about *her* ballroom antics when *she* was the mother of the "House of Labasia." The house was notoriously known as a drag diva fashion house that threw elaborate balls for the uber fabulous drag queens.

Cori Brooks was another platinum plus hairstylist who specialized in natural unprocessed hair, dread locks, and braids.

She was six-feet tall, half Caucasian and half Senegalese, and startlingly beautiful.

Then, there was Tajil, a gay butch queen. He was very handsome and had a masculine physique from long hours in the gym. The guy had a body to die for and no obvious homosexual traits, but he was sweeter than a can of cream. He was known for his sharp haircuts and could convince Rapunzel to cut her hair. He was nasty with the shears and after the initial shock of the cut, his customers were always satisfied with the results.

Last but not least was Ms. Mary. She was the mother of Star Status Styles. She kept the salon running smoothly for Miosha. She was from the old school and could lay a relaxer down making the kinkiest hair texture silky, roller set, like a Dominican; and, color like she gave birth to Ms. Clairol. She was also Miosha's grandmother and the reason she decided to open the salon. When Miosha retired from modeling she was all set to jet set around the world and enjoy her life, but unfortunately Ms. Mary, her loving sixty-two-year old nana had lost her home and beauty parlor in the Hurricane Katrina natural disaster. She was one of the thousands of displaced people after the catastrophe. She was from St. Parish, Mississippi and after she lost everything she had nowhere to go. Miosha was her only hope.

Her husband Albert died in their home. He needed insulin for his diabetes and couldn't survive the ten days it took the rescue crew to save them. He died in Ms. Mary's arms. Miosha immediately flew Ms. Mary to Atlanta and basically brought her back from the brink of insanity by opening the salon to keep her busy. She spent close to a million dollars in reconstruction and design. Six months later StarStatus Styles was born and Ms. Mary survived. Everyone at the salon and most of the clients knew about her tragedy and they all catered to her and treated her with love and the utmost respect. When Daisy stepped into the large, airy, marble foyer she squealed with delight as soon as she saw Ms. Mary "You look great Nana. I love what you did to your hair." gushed Daisy. She adored the elderly lady and looked up to her as if she was her grandmother.

"Thanks, sugar, you like it? Labasia did it for me," she blushed, patting her freshly weaved do. "That chile had me cutting up while I was in his—oops—I mean "her" chair," she stammered as her honey complexion turned red. She always got confused when it came to Labasia's sexuality.

"That's alright, just remember how fabtastic I am and all thoughts of a man will vanish when it comes to me, Miss Thang," teased Labasia in her over the top drag queen banter. Everyone in the salon cracked up with laughter.

Anjel marveled at the sight of the gigantic crystal chandelier that dazzled her every time she entered the chic salon. She admired the gold gilded mirrors that covered the walls of each stylist station. She felt like royalty every time she stepped on the Italian marble floors Miosha had imported from Italy. The salon's decorative theme was Louis XIV. The stylist chairs were custom made French provincial salon seats. All the styling equipment was gold plated except for Ms. Mary's—she preferred her special cast iron curling iron that she managed to salvage from the wreckage of her old shop. The tools were an eyesore and didn't compliment the décor of the salon. Miosha let her keep them considering the circumstances—she felt so bad for her grandmother and grieved with her for her grandfather.

Miosha was a stunningly beautiful woman—she had a pretty cinnamon complexion with high cheekbones. Her distinguished features gave her the aristocratic look of a Native American Princess. She stood 6'2" and had the svelte shape necessary to claim super-model status. She wore a short silky blonde wig over her naturally long hair but was known for her various hairstyles. Whatever the look was she wore it well. Daisy adored Miosha and looked up to her like a big sister. Miosha greeted the girls with air kisses "Look at my fabulous little sisters what are you divas up to?"

"We stopped by for a little pampering. We had a hard day," giggled Daisy

"Doing what, pray tell?" asked Miosha knowing good and well the girls didn't do anything more strenuous than lifting their champagne glasses to toast at a party or shop and that hardly constituted as a hard day.

"My hands hurt from carrying shopping bags around the mall," Daisy joked, cracking herself up with laughter. Anjel laughed and smacked Daisy five.

"Work. You fly ass divas," shouted Labasia, snapping her hands in a zigzag fashion. Everybody laughed at Labasia's dramatic antics. It was a typical day at the salon everyone was busy with clients. The giant flat screen hung on the wall like a priceless piece of artwork and was playing videos on 106 and park. "Ooh, I love Keyshia Cole's weave. That shit is hot. The two-toned blonde and burnt orange are so unique," said Anjel, turning to Labasia. "I want that."

106 and Park were playing flashback videos and the singer Keyshia Cole was singing her heart out.

"Alright miss honey-your-wish-is-my-command, go upstairs and pick out your hair, tell Chino to match your texture and blend your colors," Labasia instructed her, referring to the in-house wig and weaving hair factory located on the premises. Anjel was excited. She loved getting her hair hooked up. "Darling run along and get the hair so I can transform you from a pumpkin to a princess," teased the transvestite.

"As long as you have me done before midnight, *Fairy* Godmother," Anjel snapped back, sarcastically putting the emphasis on fairy.

"Touche," Labasia said, blowing Anjel a kiss. Daisy chuckled and shook her head at the two of them. They loved each other, but Labaisa couldn't help being a shady cunt. It's what made her Labasia.

"Love never knew what I been missing till I found LOOOVEEE..." crooned Labasia, singing along with Keyshia Cole.

"Shut up, hag. You sound like a dying rooster," Tajil snapped at Labasia.

"Ooo, whats eating you, Miss Thang?" quipped Labasia sassily.

"Nothing I just hate when you ruin a good song. Let that chile sing—that's my song," Tajil rolled his eyes annoyed by Labasia's antics.

"Now, now be nice boys," Ms. Mary lovingly reprimanded them.

"I'm always nice, Nana, but that fierce queen is annoying," Tajil whined, sounding every bit the homosexual that he was.

"Have a seat Daisy," Ms. Mary patted her chair signaling for Daisy to sit. "Baby I love your hair—it's so healthy," She said ignoring Tajil's temper tantrum.

"It's because of you, Nana, you keep my hair so beautiful." She wished they would change the channel on the flat screen. She felt bad enough and the last thing she needed was a sappy love song blaring in her ears while she tried to relax and pamper herself. Just seeing Tyrese's blazing ass who played Keisha Cole's lover in the video made her reminisce, especially the scene where they are shopping in the store, or the part when the cops pulled Keisha over and didn't ticket her because he was star struck.

Daisy had a similar situation when she drove Chio's phantom and was pulled over. Young Chio rolled his window down and gave the cop his autograph in lieu of not getting a ticket. She missed Chio already, but she knew it was over. She couldn't compete with the nasty shit the freak Kitty was probably doing to him. Knowing that freak, she gave him her ass and everything. Daisy was no fool that's why he hadn't called her yet. Her heart ached but she felt better about robbing his cheating ass. *I hope he catches something from her stank ass,* thought Daisy as she lowered her head into the basin so Ms. Mary could wash and message her stress away.

CHAPTER 9

Anthony parked in the salon's parking lot waiting patiently for Daisy to emerge when he saw his cousins pull up. "What up cuz?" he called out to Coco as she and Casey got out and unloaded their stolen goods.

"Oh shit, Mr. NBA—what you doing in town?" grinned Coco rushing him with a wild bear hug. "What are you doing here? You got a chick in the Salon?" Casey asked him as she shoved Coco over for some love from her famous cousin.

"Damn, y'all still as nosy as ever I see and what the hell is that shit in your trunk? Don't tell me y'all stealing shit again?" Anthony asked in disgust. "I give you girls an allowance plus I bought y'all a nice house out here and y'all still stealing? What the hell is wrong with you?"

"Chillax big cuz we bought some stuff and when we ran out of money we picked up a few things, but it's not that serious," Coco rationalized.

"We spent a lot of money. We deserve to buy one get one free," cracked Casey, trying a lame joke hoping to calm Anthony down.

The girls burst out laughing and continued to crack jokes and tease their cousin until he finally gave up and laughed with the silly twins.

"I know what, if you two badasses get caught I'm letting you rot in jail," he warned half serious. He shook his head and marveled at the pretty twins. They had everything that they wanted and it was still not good enough. The twins grew up with him and when his mom moved down south her sister and children followed. Their families are very close and since the twins have no brothers he acted as big bro and cousin.

The twins were enrolled at Georgia Tech University and he had to make a hefty contribution to get them in. Academically they qualified, but their behavior was horrendous. The girls were hell raisers. It was rare to find a set of identical twins which had identical personalities. Usually one was good and the other mischievous or in some cases one might be outgoing and the other shy. Coco and Casey were the exceptions in both cases.

Both girls were menaces to society. They have very high IQs so the school couldn't deny them, but their criminal behavior in their previous high school preceded them. There was an unsolved case of arson lingering on their records along with shop lifting, credit card fraud, and assault. Casey almost went to prison for setting the girl who cut Coco's face on fire. The police couldn't prove it because they never figured out which twin did it. They drove their family crazy but they are so cute and innocent looking that they got away with murder. They could manipulate their way out of anything.

Coco was 4'11" and her twin was exactly the same height. They both wore a petite size zero women with their hair in blonde braided extensions styled in side ponytails. Coco favored hers on the right side and Casey rocked hers on the left. The girls have flawless beige complexions with big Diana Ross eyes and lush lashes. The demure girls were often compared to the Olsen twins because of their elfin stature. They also favored little angels which made it difficult for Anthony to stay mad at them.

Before Coco was viciously slashed across her face you couldn't tell them apart and luckily for her, the scar which runs from her ear to her chin is barely noticeable. The cut blended neatly into her smooth skin. Nevertheless, Coco was still self-conscience and hated to look at that side of her face. Casey almost wanted to cut her own face so her best friend and beloved twin could feel better about herself. The sisters were inseparable from birth. They used to dress identically but stopped after Coco got cut they couldn't pull the ole switcheroo anymore so it was pointless.

"Listen, brats I want y'all to take care of something for me," he devised a plan as soon as he spotted his cousins. "It's this chick in that salon that I want to get at. She did some grimy shit to me and I want her touched."

"What's the bitch name?" Casey asked anxious to whoop a bitch ass for her cousin.

"Her name is Daisy Jones," Anthony spat on the ground as he said her name.

"Daisy Jones," Casey yelled. "We just saw her in the mall. She looked out for us while we stole some shit in the mall."

"So what if she violated Ant she gotta get it," Coco stated matter of factly.

"I know, I know. I'm just saying I dig her. She's mad cool. Plus, she spends a lot of bread with us. But fuck dat hoe. If she fucked with big cuz she's a done deal." shrugged Casey. It was out of her hands. Her loyalties were to Anthony and she was ready to do whatever to Daisy.

"Hold up killers," teased Anthony "I don't want y'all to do nothing to the broad. I can't afford to let anything happen to you guys—Auntie would kill me. I just want y'all to get next to her and find out where she lives, start hanging out with her and keep me posted on her moves. I'll handle the rest," Anthony plotted devilishly.

"Oh, that's easy—she loves us. She always wants us to roll with her, but we're too busy," said Coco.

"Well free up for a minute and spend some time with her so you can get me the info I need."

"We got you, cuz. We'll have that info for you by tonight or at the latest tomorrow," said Coco confidently.

"That's what's up. I can always count on you two double boogers," Anthony teased as he leaned out the window of the truck and pulled both their ponytails playfully "Yo, here, put this in your pockets," he said and dug into his jeans and pulled out a thick wad of bills. He tossed the money clip at Casey and winked at the girls as he pulled off. "Holla at me when you get that."

"We love you, Blackie," sang the twins, teasing their favorite cousin, calling him his childhood nickname.

The girls were ecstatic that he hit them off with the money and immediately began fighting over it.

"How much is it?" asked Coco rushing her twin to count the wad of cash.

"Wait a minute, girl. Damn, your thirsty ass." snapped Casey playfully, sucking her teeth as she counted the hundred dollar bills quickly and came up with four thousand dollars.

"Good, it's an even split. Gimme my deuce," demanded Coco.

"Here, crackhead," Casey teased her twin for acting like a fiend.

"This is the easiest two grand I ever made. He could have given me a hundred and I would have whooped Daisy's Ass," quipped Coco.

"Who you telling, I like honey, but blood is thicker than any chick, she fucked with the wrong nigga," hissed Casey as she rolled her eyes and smirked.

"Be cool, fool, we can't let her catch on that we're not feeling her," warned Coco.

"I know. And, who you calling a fool?" snapped Casey.

The twins waltzed into the Salon eager to begin their mission. "Hey," they sang in unison. "We got some goodies for you Divas up in here," Coco sing-songed jovially. She knew the staff and the clients loved when they came thru with hot merchandise to sell. Everybody likes a bargain.

"Oooh, girls come to mama. I got my coins ready to spend," Labasia called out to the girls, trying to lure them to her station so "she" could get first dibs at the goods.

"Uh um, Ms. Thang, I already got first choice. Don't I twins?" Daisy asked the sisters smugly, she knew she was priority since she looked out for them in the store. She wanted the *Christian Louboutin* shoes she noticed had disappeared from the display as she was leaving the store. She wore a size seven and knew the shoes were her size her small, pretty feet always fit the display shoes.

"Labasia, we got you, boo. But Daisy is right. She does get first dibs. She looked out for us. We owe her," Coco smiled warmly at Daisy. Daisy smiled as she scrambled through the bag of goodies. She spotted the stilettos became moist.

"I definitely want these and I'll take both pairs of those *Dereon* jeans." She loved Beyonce's line of denims—they fit her heart shaped booty and small waist perfectly.

"Tell you what," Casey chirped, "you can have this whole bag of stuff for a thousand dollars Daisy." She was ecstatic because the shoes alone retailed for nine hundred dollars so she was basically paying for one pair and getting two pairs of three hundred dollar jeans along with three sexy Dolce & Gabbana tops that ran four hundred a pop. *Damn*, she thought she was getting eighteen hundred dollars worth of clothes for free. She loved the twins.

"Aw, that's so sweet of y'all," gushed, Daisy. "Soon as Anjel and I finish our hair, let's go kick it at the jungle," she offered, falling right into the twin's trap.

"That's what's up, Daisy, we can hang wit y'all tonight—how 'bout we meet at your crib so we can all roll together?"

"It's gonna be crazy finding parking so we can ride together in my truck," said Coco. She drove an extra long Tahoe it was true about lil' girls liking big things. They could have a party in her ride.

"That's cool, I'm tired anyway and I don't feel like driving. I'll call you with my address when I get home," said Daisy.

Bingo, Casey thought.

"All set we're going to head home to get dressed," offered Coco, giddy because she fell into their trap so easily.

"Hey, Ms. Mary, we got you something too."

"What you got for me, baby?" cooed Ms. Mary, smiling with anticipation. Coco rummaged thru her purse and produced a bottle of Kimora Lee's perfume Goddess.

"Ah, thanks, sugar." Nana was so grateful she pecked both of the twins on their cheeks with kisses. "Such sweet pretty young ladies," she said.

"Thank you, ma'am," the little fakers said in unison, If only Ms. Mary knew how devilish the girls really were.

"What about me? Don't Labasia get anything?" sniffed the transvestite, upset at the snub. "Hell, what am I? chopped meat. My money 'spend just as long as Daisy's," interrupted Tajil angrily.

Cori looked at the girls and shook her head in disgust. She was one of the few that didn't approve of the girls stealing shenanigans and certainly wasn't going to help support their criminal activities.

"You girls should be ashamed of yourselves. You're college students for Christ sakes. You should be studying, not stealing," chastised Cori. "You're going to get busted and ruin your lives," she continued to berate them.

"There are two girls in my psychology class that strip for a living. Would you rather we be known as the wonder twins down at Magic's?" Coco asked sarcastically.

"No, I'd rather you get a decent job and struggle legally, instead of breaking the law," replied Cori curtly. "And furthermore you guys aren't helping them by buying their stolen goods," she said as she glared around the salon. Everybody quickly avoided her accusing stare and got back to work, after all, she was right.

"You're right Ms. Cori, we plan to quit boosting as soon as we finish paying for our mother's operation. There is a substantial amount left on the bill that her insurance won't cover," said Casey dramatically. She was lying thru her teeth and doing a damn good job. She could have got an academy award for the performance. Their mother was perfectly healthy. She wanted Cori to get off their backs, so she went for the sympathy route. She went as far as squeezing out a few tears.

"I didn't know your mother was sick," Cori said, immediately remorseful.

"We don't like to discuss her illness, but we need extra money to help with her bills and our tuition," Coco chimed in glibly, quickly add-libbing her sister's lie. She wasn't expecting the extreme tale but she was used to her sister's performances. She could always get them out of a jam with her quick game she was so good at running on people.

"Oh Gawd. That's awful." gasped Labasia. Suddenly the entire salon was offering the twins condolences and hugs.

"Well, babies I will pray for your mother. I know my Alfred is with the Lord waiting for me, but I can't leave my Miosha just yet," said Ms. Mary all choked up over the girls' plight.

"You better not, Nana," Miosha admonished her grandmother. *OK, it's time to cut the shit—it's getting too mushy*, Coco thought, feeling guilty for making Ms. Mary sad. Casey was giddy on the inside although she maintained a sad face. She knew Daisy would really let her guard down now—she trusted them completely. Nothing beats a good sob story. As if on cue Daisy grabbed Casey in a tight bear hug.

"If you need anything, I got y'all, in fact, here is another thousand dollars. You girls can't afford to give up deals right now." She shoved the money in Casey's hand before she could say no. Knowing that she had no intention of giving anything back she pocketed the cash and continued on with her performance. Coco gave her dramatic twin a look which meant cut the drama it was time to leave. She hated to deceive Ms. Mary, but she had to get the bitch Cori off their case and out of their business. Anthony would be proud of how easy they had Daisy in the palm of their hands. If Cori only knew they stole because they loved the excitement. It was an adrenaline rush much like extreme sports. They hardly needed the money. Anthony made sure they were well cared for. He looked out for his entire family. She was happy they never mentioned that they were related to the baller, the gig would have been up. Besides they would think they were crazy if they knew that their millionaire cousin gave them allowances and they still took things that didn't belong to them.

"OK, we're gone. Hit me on my cell, Daisy, when y'all are ready for us to pick you up."

"OK, see you in a bit," replied Daisy. The game had just begun the twins left the salon eager to call Anthony.

CHAPTER 10

Kitty was in her glory. She was in Chio's mansion. He had brought her home and she had no intentions of leaving. Young Chio wanted to record her in his home studio. Everything was moving extremely fast and she was thrilled. 48 hours ago she was shaking her ass to his songs in the strip club, now she was inside of his home ready to record a song of her own. She could have jumped for joy if she wasn't so sore from their wild freak session, which was the reason she made it to Chio's mansion—she fucked his ass silly. She had that *glooey-pooey*. That was what she called her pussy because whoever gets in it gets stuck.

She giggled to herself as she fixed her makeup in Chio's lavish bedroom. It was the size of her bedroom complete with a stand-up steam shower stall and a Jacuzzi the size of a mini pool. She had never seen anything like it, it could seat twenty people—there was a built-in sixty-inch flat screen covering the wall and a built-in mini bar. *Whew, this boy is living the life,* she thought, glancing around the bathhouse. It certainly wasn't an ordinary bathroom. She noticed a pair of thongs with decorative rhinestones shaped like a daisy flower. She lifted the offensive undergarments off the crystal water sprout with two fingers and flung them in the garbage. *Daisy Jones is history,* she thought. *I'll kill that puta before I let my papi chulo go.* She fluffed her curls in the mirror and daydreamed about living with him in his 21,000-square feet. mansion.

He had 12 acres of land and a fortress that surrounded his estate. She felt her pussy creaming at the thought of being the mistress of his lavish palace. He had ten bedrooms which she planned to freak-off in each and every one of them. His layout included eleven bathrooms, a movie theater, basketball court, bowling alley, pool room plus two Olympic size pools, one indoor and one out. The mansion housed forty-five rooms all together including an elevator. Young Chio was balling out of control. Her panties were soaked by the time she snapped out of her trance. He knocked on the door right on time.

"Mami, what you up to?" inquired Chio, strolling into the bathroom and pressed up against Kitty's ass, she snuggled against his body and started grinding her butt against his groin. "Oh you ain't have enough yet?" asked Chio incredulously. *Damn this freak is one hot number,* he thought, bugging over how horny she was even after their marathon sex session. He forgot how frisky Latin women were and wasn't about to disappoint her even though his dick was so chafed he felt like his skin was going to fall off. He had no choice but to give her his tongue. He usually saved that treat for his special lady which currently happened to be Daisy. *What the hell,* he thought. Kitty was going to contribute to his fortune when he made her a superstar.

He lifted her up on the marble counter of his sink and placed her in the doggy style position as he licked kitty's juicy p bone until she screamed and bucked her fat ass in his face, blasting him with her cum. He rubbed his face back and forth in her wet throbbing pussy and shook his dreads wildly. Damn, she was tasty. He smeared her juices all over his nose, savoring her fresh scent. She tasted just as good as Daisy, which was impressive, considering Daisy had that virgin fresh off the press pussy. Yeah, Kitty was a keeper. He wondered if he could have them both. He still wanted to be the first to tap Daisy's p-bone. He felt like she owed him that privilege. He had to figure out a way to make her accept Kitty. One of them five-carat pink diamond rings might do it. Yeah, he would buy her a ring and make her see what she would be missing if she decided to leave him. After all, no one ever left him—he was Young Chio the self- made millionaire. That's what they heralded him as on the cover of *Rolling Stone* magazine. His story was similar to a few of the other independent record label owners except for a slight twist. Baby and Slim from *Cash Money* and Master P had a lot in common with Chio they were all southern men who grew up in poverty and overcame the obstacles to become very successful millionaires. The only difference with Chio was he didn't deal drugs or claim a gangsta lifestyle. His come up was very different. He was a professional stud, a kept man. In other words, he screwed his way to the top.

At an early age, he realized that he was gifted with a talent. He had an extra large penis and a charming way with women. By the time he was sixteen, he had slept with all his mother's friends and three of his high school teachers. Women loved him, especially older ones. He had a sugar mama named, Ms. Lilly who financed his career. His mother worked for her as a housekeeper and sometimes she brought Chio to work with her.

He had free reign to run around the enormous estate while his mom cleaned and prepared meals for Ms. Lilly. One day when he was twelve he accidentally barged into Ms. Lilly's bedroom and discovered her legs spread wide while she stroked herself with a vibrator. He immediately became aroused. Although he was still a virgin at the time, he was beginning puberty and his hormones were going bonkers. He wanted to fuck Ms. Lilly. When she noticed him standing in her doorway she motioned for him to come to her. Chio didn't hesitate—he skipped over to her king size sleigh bed and kindly hopped into bed with her. With no words spoken between them, she replaced the vibrator with his enormous penis.

Ms. Lilly was a very attractive middle-aged white woman with a very large bank account. Her husband had recently passed away and she was happy the old geezer was gone. He was a tyrant and he never satisfied her in bed. He was so mean that she had his remains burned to a crisp and placed in an urn that she used as an ashtray. It sat on the floor by her bed.

She was excited by the size of Young Chios penis and she conveniently ignored the fact that he was twelve years old and the son of her housekeeper. She had never seen a penis that large on an adult much less on a child. She had never been with a Negro and was turned on. She justified the molestation by telling him she was teaching him the proper way to have sex. She sucked and fucked Young Chio with abandon. While his mother unknowingly polished her marble kitchen floors, Ms. Lilly taught Chio everything he needed to know about pleasing a woman. She also took very good care of him. When he wanted his own record label she gave him the start-up money, forking over a hundred thousand of her dead husband's money happily. Young Chio serviced her sexual needs for years and she showed her appreciation by spoiling him rotten. She even retired his mother early and bought her a beautiful house. The housekeeper was so happy she never realized why her boss was being so generous. Chio made sure Ms. Lilly took care of his mama and what he wanted he got. On his 19th birthday, she bought him a fully remodeled 88' Impala, his favorite old school ride and a check for 100,000 to build his studio. The rest was history.

Kitty was still cumming from the sensational head Chio gave her. She was so happy she could bust. "Papi, what do you want me to sing for you?" She composed herself as she adjusted the microphone and sat in his state of the art recording booth. Her nipples were hard from the after flush of sex and she was butt ass naked. Chio thought it would be fun to have her sing in her birthday suit. He engineered and produced his music, so he wasn't worried about anybody seeing her they had total privacy in his studio. He sat at his mixing board naked, absently stroking his penis while contemplating the lyrics he wanted her to sing on his hook.

"OK, Mami, I got it. I want you to ride this here beat and flow wit' it and sing the lyrics like you in love wit' a nigga." He taught her the song and she laid the track down in five takes which were exceptional. Kitty never felt so erotic and sexy while singing. She caressed her body and rubbed her private parts with each high note she hit. Chio was pleased with her performance. She was a true professional and very marketable. He decided to photograph her in the booth singing naked with the headphones on her head and her long curls covering her breast. The concept was priceless he knew he would sell off her image alone. Having talent was a plus in the music industry, but it was more so about sex appeal and image. Kitty had the *it* factor and with the money he had for her marketing campaign, there was no way she could lose. She had movie star appeal and reminded him of a Penelope Cruz with a touch of Selma Hayek. Both of the Latina actresses were very hot. He made love to Kitty again before heading to his club to celebrate her first single. He instructed Kitty to go to Daisy's closet and pick an outfit to wear. He paid for the pricey designer gear and figured if he wanted his artist to wear an outfit, Daisy shouldn't mind. Kitty grinned as she picked thru the new gear that would soon belong to her.

CHAPTER 11

Coco pulled up in front of Daisy's house she lived in Bankhead, West Atlanta. It wasn't a plush neighborhood, but the houses were decent. The neighborhood was called *The Trap* popularized by T.I., the self-proclaimed King of the south. Mama Jones used his construction company to rehab her house. She and the rapper's grandmother were neighbors. Daisy loved T.I. like a cousin and he adored her. They grew up together.

"Casey ring Daisy's jack and tell her we're outside," Coco nudged her twin who was fiddling with the CD changer.

"You call her. What's wrong with your hands?" snapped Casey.

"Girl just do it," ordered Coco. She was older by four minutes and took the older sister thing seriously, demanding respect from her younger twin.

"Alright, damn, I was just playing," pouted Casey.

MACK MAMA

"That's your problem you play too much. This ain't a game. We need to be on point tonight. We got her address, but we still need to rock her to sleep in case we have to handle her for Blackie."

"'Aight, I'm hitting her phone now," sulked Casey.

Shortly after, Anjel and Daisy strutted out of the house dressed to kill. They rocked the latest fashion from their favorite designers. Daisy had on a Christian Dior white bikini top with a matching leather mini skirt. Anjel wore Roberto Cavalli with some tiny shorts that flattered her butt. Her ass cheeks were spilling out of the teeny shorts, both of the girls' exuded sex appeal. The twins were impressed, but they knew they looked sensational as well, so they weren't bothered they had on matching Chanel dresses. Casey's was white and form-fitting with the logo embossed on the front of her dress. Coco wore black and had the same design. The dresses were skin tight and fit the girls like a second skin they both wore their hair down so it was impossible to tell them apart. "Oooh, you two look gorgeous," squealed Daisy.

"Yup it's going down tonight we're going to turn that motherfucker out," hooted Anjel. All four of the girls cracked up and took off to the club in great spirits. Daisy hoped to bump into Chio. She planned to ignore him and flirt with the first baller she saw to make him jealous.

As soon as they entered the Jungle, Daisy spotted Chio and Kitty. "I Know that ain't that ho Kitty sitting on Chio's lap," stuttered Daisy nearly choking on her own saliva.

"No, that Bitch ain't up in here with your man," instigated Anjel.

"And that skank got on my new Dolce & Gabbana dress Chio bought me," whispered Daisy in disbelief.

"No, that bitch didn't," spat Anjel.

"That trifling nigga let her go up in my closet." Daisy was flabbergasted and could hardly believe her eyes. Kitty was holding court like she was the queen of Sheba in the V.I.P. section of the club. She began slow dancing with Chio suggestively while Mack Mama's sexy song, *Dance On,* was playing. She was grinding on him and rubbing on his neck. Daisy was fuming. She wanted to kill Chio and beat the blood out of Kitty, but she had to hold her composure or Chio would have her thrown out of his club furthering her embarrassment. No one had ever disrespected Daisy like that or cheated on her for that matter and she didn't know how to take it. Chio had downright shitted on her and to add insult to injury he was parading around with the bitch in public. Daisy was crushed.

"Get outta here, Daisy, you were messing with Young Chio?" Casey gasped in awe. The twins were impressed that Daisy was dating the richest dude in Atlanta and found all the drama exciting. They immediately began rubbing it in.

"If that was me and another chick played me like that I would bring it to her ass," Coco said egging Daisy on.

"I'm going to kill that bitch." Daisy's voice echoed over the loud music. Several females turned in their direction startled by Daisy's outburst.

"Well?" Coco glared at the partygoers. The girls smirked and quickly looked away unwilling to mess up their perfect hairdo's scuffling with Coco. She was little but the glint in her eyes warned of the danger that lived inside of her, she would have jumped on the prissy girls like a wild monkey and Casey would have been on them like a fly on shit.

"I don't feel like fighting, or let me rephrase that, fucking nobody up tonight, sis. I'm not trying to get nobody's blood on my dress," stated Casey nonchalantly.

"Yo, Daisy what you wanna do to that bitch? We got your back ma." offered Coco.

"First of all let's go up in V.I.P. so I can check his ass. I'll deal with that tramp later," Daisy said as she stormed through the crowd with the girls trailing closely behind her. They were stopped abruptly by a bodyguard blocking the roped off area. "Baby, Young Chio is expecting us and he wouldn't like it if we didn't show up. A party ain't a party if we're not in the building." Daisy licked her lips suggestively. Anjel and the twins followed suit, each one enticing the bouncer with their sexiness. A second later they were in V.I.P. Chio and Kitty was hugged up in the corner surrounded by buckets of fine champagne cluttering the table. Daisy blew a gasket and finally lost control, she marched over and snatched a bottle up and smashed it over Kitty's head.

"Ooowww." Kitty moaned loudly, startled by the pain "What the Fuck?" she said Kitty, clutching her head trying to stop the blood that gushed from her skull.

"Bitch, are you nuts?" asked Chio.

"No, nigga, iz you crazy? You got this cheap whore up in my shit and flaunting her in my face," Daisy said hysterically. Anjel and the twins stood in shock. They were stunned by Daisy's outburst and just as surprised as Chio and Kitty. She hadn't prepared them for her spontaneous attack—blood trickled down Kitty's face and dripped on her dress or rather Daisy's dress. "Bitch you getting blood on my dress." screeched Daisy. Chio suddenly snapped and back smacked the shit out of Daisy. He hit her so hard she felt her lip bust as she stumbled against her friends.

"Hoe, don't you ever disrespect me or my artist again. She got on *my* dress that I bought for any piece of ass I want in it," Chio roared right before hog spitting in Daisy's face.

Daisy slowly wiped the glob of spit as it slid down her cheek and then she went crazy, she tried to scratch Chio's eyes out, but his bouncers managed to pull her off of him.

"I'm gonna get you, motherfucker," she yelled as she was roughly hoisted over the giant bouncer's shoulder and unceremoniously dumped on the ground outside of the club. Her friends quickly helped her up and got her in the truck. They wanted to get her home before any more drama popped off.

"Damnnnn. Daisy, you crazy, Ma. But fuck that, I would have done the same thing" Coco said, excitedly amped up over the action at the club.

"Yeah, girl, fuck dat nigga what's next?" Anjel asked knowing Daisy well enough to know it was hardly over.

"Take me home I need to think," replied Daisy, numb from the pain and humiliation. She was mortified. She couldn't believe that Chio had spit on her and worse in front of the whole club, her heart was bleeding she literally felt the punctured holes in her heart ripping away.

The girls made it to Daisy's house in record time. The twins were amped up replaying the drama over and over again. They couldn't wait to tell Anthony what happened.

"Yo, Daisy you crazy girl why didn't you tell us you were going to cold cock shorty over the head with a bottle like that." laughed Coco.

"Yeah." chimed Casey "That shit was wild until dude spit on you. If those big ass bouncers weren't protecting him we would have helped you beat his country ass down." As mad as she was Daisy started laughing at the twins they were so funny.

"Girl that's right, laugh that shit off, cuz you got up in Kitty's ass good. That slut is gonna have headaches for days and Chio's ass gonna get his, watch." pouted Anjel she was just as upset as Daisy she could feel her best friends pain.

"I know, I know. Y'all go on back to the club and tell me what happened. I hope that bitch don't yap off her mouth about me to the police," said Daisy, she didn't want to go to jail over the shit, It was so much blood gushing from Kitty's head that she knew she would need at least a hundred stitches. Daisy could be facing some serious jail time.

"OK honey, I will call you and let you know." Anjel leaned over and pecked Daisy on the cheek, hugging her tightly. "I got your back girl," she whispered in her ear. That small gesture touched Daisy. She squeezed her friend tightly and got out of the ride as a tear rolled down her face. She was in a daze as she walked into her house—never before had she felt that type of pain. She hated Kitty and Chio and wouldn't rest until she got them back for causing her heart to hurt so badly.

CHAPTER 12

"Get the fuck outta here. She did what?" Anthony couldn't believe the shit that took place at Chio's club. Daisy was wilding out over that nigga which brought him to the conclusion that her actions could only mean one thing. She gave him some pussy. He was enraged. "I'll call you back. Y'all did good. I gotta take care of something, aight." He hurried off the phone and sank down into his leather sofa he was fucked up in the head. How dare she play him like that. She had the nerve to extort him for dating her young ass, but then she goes and fucks his homie? Anthony vowed to destroy Daisy's grimy ass.

* * *

"Yo, I' ain't gonna front that chick, Daisy Jones ain't no punk. I ain't know shorty had heart like that. But you know these country broads are known for getting crunk in da clubs," said Casey, recalling how Daisy ran up on Kitty.

"Yeah she fucked shorty up with that bottle, but the funniest shit was when Young Chio hog spit on her and she went bananas. It took three of them big ass bouncers to restrain her crazy ass, that's why we can't sleep on her when it's time to attack. We gotta come full force. The element of surprise is important we can't let her see it coming." Coco cracked her knuckles as she plotted on Daisy. The twins had dropped Anjel off at Magic City and were headed back to the Jungle to finish partying. When they arrived the front of the club was packed. Casey spotted Ivy, the leader of their clique *Original Bad Girls* (OBG's). Ivy was from Brooklyn, New York and lived in Forte Green Projects. The twins were from Marcy Projects which was in the same hood.

Ivy had moved to Atlanta two years before Anthony moved the girls there. They had recruited a team of boosters, pickpockets, check forgers, and credit card users that wrecked havoc in the Georgia malls. The twins idolized Ivy and was honored to be down with her.

Ivy was treacherous when it came to getting money. Anything was possible. She left New York after a robbery she was involved in went fatally wrong. She had set up a big-time drug dealer to get jacked for five-kilos of cocaine. She dated him to find out where he lived, and then managed to find out where he kept his stash. She sent her girls to the spot and they wiped him out. Unfortunately for him, he figured she was behind the robbery and when he confronted her she was forced to kill him. She fled New York and was laying low in Atlanta. Ivy was notorious for her cold-blooded antics and her multi crime sprees she was dubbed Poison Ivy because she was evil as all hell. She made a small fortune from identity theft scams and had a stable of OBG's ready to rob and kill for her.

"Hey, twins, what's good?" Ivy greeted the sisters jovially. "Y'all just getting here? You missed the show. This chick cracked Chio's artist in the head with a bottle. He put a hit out on her ass and I'm looking for Shorty. He's paying five grand for his name carved across her face," reported Ivy excitedly.

"Damn," Coco squealed. "I know where she lives. Can I get a grand for bringing her to you?"

"Yeah I will hit you off but how do you know who did it?" Ivy asked.

"Cuz, we were just in there standing right next to the broad when she cut her. Her name is Daisy Jones. We just dropped her off. Wanna go get her now? We can get her to come outside, she trusts us." Casey was already counting the thousand she and her sister would share from the hit money.

"Naw, no rush I'm chilling tonight let's go to Magic City. I gotta meet Geechi over there." Ivy was anxious to meet up with her man. She knew every woman in ATL wanted him or one of his partners. They had it going on definitely baller status, wherever he and his crew went there were literally flocks of chickens clucking around them. They called themselves, the *Black Columbian Cartel*, BCC for short. They ran shit where ever they went and were treated like celebrities. Geechi was their leader. He was half black mixed with Columbian and all his boys were bi-racial. It was over a dozen fine half Indian, half Spanish dudes in the BCC. They had a drug organization that controlled half the south and part of the Midwestern drug traffic. Coco and Casey were thrilled they never had an opportunity to hang with the popular crew and were happy to get the chance to finally meet them. Coco had a huge crush on Red, the gorgeous rapper in the crew. He had a couple of underground hits out that were buzzing in the clubs. Although he was knee deep in the drug game his record label helped the boys wash their money. "Girl, is Red going to be there?" Coco asked, squeezing Ivy's arm excitedly.

"Bitch let my arm go and I will see." Ivy shook Coco off of her and dialed Geechi's phone. He answered on the third ring.

"Talk about it," was Geechi's usual greeting.

"Hey, babe, I'm on my way. I'm bringing a few of my girls with me. Is Red there?" Ivy cooed lovingly.

"He right here," Geechi replied.

"Tell him he owes me one. I'm bringing him every man's fantasy. Twins." she laughed and clicked off the line.

"I don't know why you said that. I don't like that dude and I and my sister don't share men," snorted Casey, coping an instant attitude.

"Girl please, I tell a nigga what he wants to hear. I don't care if you fuck him or not. He's gonna break me off at the thought of sticking you double mint twins," giggled Ivy.

"I'm gonna bag that nigga tonight and I don't need Casey's help trust," replied Coco cockily.

Casey sucked her teeth and rolled her eyes in disgust. She wasn't into messing with different guys, she had a boyfriend but secretly she was attracted to women. She was anxious to get to Magic City to see the beautiful erotic dancers, not the BCC that's for sure. She liked girls since she was ten years old. It was the only secret she had ever kept from her twin. She had a brief affair with one of her female professors at school and was so paranoid that Coco would find out that she abruptly ended it. Casey was miserable and felt trapped she cared about her boyfriend, but he didn't make her feel like she did when she was with a woman. She didn't know when, but she knew eventually she would have to face who she really was and come out of the closet. *It ain't going to be tonight,* she thought as they parked their rides and entered the strip club.

Geechi had left word with the bouncers that he was expecting them so there was no waiting in the long line. They were escorted to the V.I.P section of the club reserved for heavy spenders. "It's poppin' in here tonight," Coco yelled over the loud bass blaring from the club speakers. The popular strip club was packed with rowdy rich men and a few female spectators enjoying the show with their men. The BCC filled half the club. There were at least fifty guys from the cartel in the crowded club. They rolled deep where ever they went. The dancers were elated because there was so much money in the house. The girls also knew that Geechi and his crew spent money like it was water, they let it flow and invented the term 'make it rain' when they threw buckets of hundreds and fifties at the naked women. The last time they visited Magic's every girl cleared five grand a piece. The strippers literally would fight for attention, especially from Geechi. When Ivy spotted the BCC she didn't see her man right away but then she saw something that set her blood boiling. "Who is that slut butt sitting on my baby's lap?" she seethed she was furious and dripping venom, she hated how Geechi flaunted other women in her face. He knew she was coming and should have had the decency to keep the hoe's off of him. She marched over ready to take care of the problem.

"Oh shit, that's Anjel. That's Daisy Jones' best friend. We were just with them at Jungle's," stated Coco

"I don't give a fuck who friend she is she can get it too, she better raise up off my man," said Ivy.

Anjel was working and oblivious to Ivy and the twins watching her. She seductively twirled and straddled Geechi as she gyrated erotically on his lap Ivy came up behind her and almost snatched the weave tracks out of her scalp.

"Oww. What the fuck?" Anjel shrieked in agony. Before she knew what happened Ivy had her on the ground with her razor at her neck.

"Bitch, get off my man and don't let me catch your nasty ass on him again." spat Ivy wildly.

Geechi pulled her off of Anjel roughly.

"Beech is you crazy? Sit ya ass down. Shawty doing what she gets paid to do," he growled.

Anjel jumped up ready to go off but stopped in her tracks when Geechi handed her a stack of hundreds. He patted her on her ass and told her to leave it alone. She had to respect his gangsta but she was seething inside. She glared at Ivy as she adjusted her g-string and walked away. She didn't even notice the twins.

"Ooowee you got yourself a live wire man," Red hooted laughing hysterically.

"What up lil' mama, wit' your crazy ass?" The rapper greeted Ivy with a bear hug. She pushed him off of her and confronted Geechi, unwilling to leave well enough alone, she wanted to check his ass for disrespecting her.

"Why you had that trick all up on you like that Geechi?" Ivy demanded indifferently to the ass-kicking she was sure to get for her insolence. The twins sat down quickly, leaving Ivy standing alone defiantly in front of Geechi. She had a hand on hip in her gangstress pose.

Ivy was 5'8", brown-skinned with an ordinary face. What made her stand out was her natural long hair that hung past her shoulders down the middle of her back. Other than that there was nothing special about her, she was rail thin with her height she looked like a runway model. She was a fly girl and only wore designer labels. Ivy stole only the best. Chanel and Roberto Cavalli were her favorites. She stood before Geechi furious, clad in Chanel from head to toe, as dark as it was in the club she had on her matching shades, but the glasses couldn't hide the pain in her eyes. She was hurt and it wasn't the first time Geechi had wounded her both emotionally and physically and knowing him it wouldn't be the last. She wasn't a fool—she knew he cheated on her, but she tried to ignore it because she was in love and couldn't stand the thought of leaving him or losing her position as his main girl. She wasn't having the bullshit and if she didn't love him so much she would have put a bullet in his head. Instead, she put up with his womanizing and abuse not to mention she knew if she dared try to retaliate his boys would hunt her down and torture her. Even so, she didn't hesitate to curse him out when she felt disrespected regardless of the consequences.

"Ivy sit down and enjoy the show if you came here to fuck up my night you can get going now," Geechi stated coldly. He was very cocky and knew he could have any woman if not all of them in the club and didn't have to deal with Ivy's tantrum, nor was he going to tolerate it. He was seconds from pimp-smacking her but what puzzled him and secretly turned him on about Ivy was her spunk. As many times as he put his foot up her ass, blackened her eyes or cracked a few ribs she still stood up to him. She was a tough New York broad and it turned him on. That and her independence he didn't have to spend money on her for shit like clothes. She had more outfits than most boutiques. Even though he looked out for her whenever she wanted something she rarely asked him for anything.

She was a go-getter and as much money as he had, she still lavished him with gifts. She liked to take care of her man. She basically bought him in the beginning, because she wasn't his type at all, he liked light-skinned women, usually Spanish or bi-racial women. He slept with black girls before but never had he made one his main chick. Ivy pushed up on him so hard and got what she wanted a position in his life she wasn't satisfied with being just a fuck. He really liked her style. The first time he met her was at his Bar and Grill restaurant she was selling Breitling watches and after he bought one for ten grand from her she gave him a matching ladies model for free and told him to give it to his mother from her new daughter in law. He got a kick out of her cockiness. After a couple of months of wild sex, she became his wifey. He had several women in his harem but, Ivy was the one he came home to. Sometimes he felt like she put voodoo on him—he couldn't seem to shake her. That was a year ago and times like this when she caused embarrassing scenes she made him want to dismiss her. He glared at her and she matched his stare down defiantly shooting him daggers in return.

"I'm not going anywhere don't play with me Geechi," Ivy said. It was a tense moment his boys looked on with interest wondering how their boss was going to handle the situation. Geechi was known for his quick temper and although they all knew that he loved Ivy they also knew he was going to beat her ass for the show she was putting on. He drew his hand back and smacked Ivy so hard she crashed to the floor. The twins gasped and ran over to help their friend. Red even felt sorry for her but she played her hand and got dealt with.

"You happy now?" shouted Geechi he was mad as fuck that she pushed him to hit her. Ivy got up, adjusted her clothes and sat down seething with anger but another emotion overrode her fury. She felt desire for Geechi burn deep in her loins. When he smacked her she damn near came on herself, she knew it was sick but she loved when he hit her she felt his love and passion through the pain he inflicted.

She was Geechi's woman—an honor that she would die before she gave up. She allowed him to beat her and the day she got tired of it he would be a dead man. She licked the blood from her busted lip and smiled, her arousal calming her down. Geechi saw her expression and knew what she wanted and was anxious to oblige. "Come on let me get you fixed up." He took her arm and led her to a private room reserved for lap dances. "Why you make me do you like that girl? You like this shit don't ya?" He asked Ivy, knowing the answer to his question was yes. His manhood started rising to the occasion immediately.

"Just as much as you do" she replied sassily eyeing his bulging erection, she pulled his dick out of his jeans and sank to the floor on her knees.

Anjel saw Geechi smack Ivy and smiled she felt special. The leader of the Black Columbian Cartel was protecting her. She always had a crush on Geechi but didn't think she had a chance other than being his sex toy, and now she had hope. She knew of Poison Ivy and her reputation, but Anjel didn't give a damn about those East Coast bitches. She would beat that hoe all the way back to New York. Anjel couldn't stand New Yorkers that came to her city tryna run shit. She had a trick for her, though, Geechi was going to be hers. Anjel was going to teach Ivy a good ole lesson about how Atlanta chicks got down. She wouldn't fuck her up she would fuck her man.

CHAPTER 13

"I didn't spend seventy grand in no fucking mall," Chio roared in the phone at his accountant furiously. He had just learned that seventy thousand was stolen off of his black American Express card. He had a nagging feeling Daisy was behind it. "Fax me the invoice with the charges, I'll check the purchases and see if I can come up with the culprit," Chio instructed his accountant. He was going to hurt Daisy's ass— she violated big time. He clicked off with his accountant and texted Poison Ivy. He wanted his initials carved in Daisy's face. It had been twenty-four hours after she showed her ass in his club and he was still pissed off. Kitty had to get fifty stitches. If her face would have been disfigured he would have put Daisy in a body bag. Kitty was an investment and he wasn't going to let Daisy's young ass fuck up his money. He didn't find the attack on Kitty amusing at all and wanted to beat fire out of Daisy for embarrassing him in his own club. He was over her. Kitty had it going on and he intended to push her project forward and make her a superstar. Daisy Jones could keep her stingy ass P-bone, snickered Chio. He had him a bonafide freak. He was going to make Daisy pay for robbing him and fucking with his bitch. No female had ever played him like a duck nigga and he didn't like feeling like a sucker.

He picked up his cell and dialed Ivy's number "Eh shawty what's happening? What's the verdict on that hoe Daisy Jones?" asked Chio impatiently he wanted results.

"Oh what up, Chio? I'm gonna get on it later I was at Magic's all night with Geechi. After I left your spot I got caught up with him, but I'm gonna handle that for you fo' sure," Ivy reassured him. She didn't tell him she was too sore from the beating Geechi gave her once they reached his crib. After they left Magic's they continued their sadistic freak session which left Ivy black and blue but strangely satisfied.

She fell deeper in love with Geechi. She loved to fight because the makeup sex was so gratifying. Ivy knew how she felt was wrong but she couldn't control her urges and didn't understand why she liked to be dominated. Every man she ever loved physically abused her. She was drawn to violence. It was because she witnessed her mother suffer for years in a bizarre abusive relationship. Her mother was murdered when Ivy was ten years old by her boyfriend. They fought constantly and made up by indulging in drugs and wild sex. Ivy could remember hearing her mother's moans and whimpers thru the thin walls of their project apartment. She was nine years old and felt obscenely aroused by the sounds of the vicious smacks her mother's man laid on her mother followed by the carnal animal grunts of their sex.

One night she peaked her head in the bedroom her curiosity getting the best of her, the vulgar scene she witnessed scarred her for life. Her mother was tied to the bed bleeding from a deep gash on her face. She whimpered while her boyfriend fucked her savagely. Ivy met her mom's vacant gaze and felt her pain but oddly she wanted to trade places with her. Her naïve innocent mind mistook the savagery for love. She thought her mother enjoyed the abuse because she made no attempts to leave him, so it was normal and therefore what Ivy expected in a relationship. Her mother even encouraged Ivy to treat her abusive lover nicely. Everything was fine as long as he continued to feed her the white powder that she loved to put in her nose. It made her sleepy. Ivy later realized that her mother was addicted to Heroin. After her mother died from an overdose combined with her last brutal beating Ivy still had no idea that what she witnessed her mom go through was not normal. She longed for a man to love her enough to beat her and make love to her. At thirty she still felt that way and put up with Geechi's violent physical abuse with a smile on her face. Geechi thought she was nuts but went on with the sick game they played enjoying the masochistic relationship. Ivy sighed as she hung up the phone. She had a job to do. She couldn't wait to take care of Daisy for Chio. Violence was second nature to her and she loved nothing more than to give and receive a good ass kicking.

She was turned on by the thought of ripping thru Daisy's soft skin with her razor. She would carve her like a Thanksgiving turkey. Ivy giggled at the gruesome thought and called the twins. It was time to go to war and her little soldiers would help her form a trap for Daisy. She took a deep drag of her blunt and began scheming.

CHAPTER 14

Daisy couldn't stop crying as she sunk deep into her down filled mattress. She curled into a fetal position and balled her eyes out. How could he? She bawled, she never felt so humiliated and especially in front of her girls. They looked up to her and now they looked at her with pity and that shit burned her up. She recalled cracking Kitty upside her head and had to laugh—she hadn't planned on losing her cool but she was hurting so bad that she lost it.

"Girl, why you in here leaking like a faucet?" Mama Jones yelled, startling Daisy so bad she nearly fell out of her bed. Her mother barged in her room glaring at her. Her intuition told her Daisy was crying over a man and she wasn't having it, no child of hers would be weak over no man. Mama Jones was as ugly as her daughter was beautiful. She stood 5'8" with broad shoulders and a strong back built for carrying babies. Back in her day, she had the baddest Coco-Cola bottle shape. But after having six kids, she was shaped like a half-gallon milk carton. She was very resentful for being out of shape. She loved her children but raised them with tough love. Daisy was the prettiest and oldest of her girls and she taught her to be ruthless when it came to dealing with men. She knew early on that Daisy would be the breadwinner for the family, her white no good daddy gave Mama a gift before he took off, and that was a beautiful daughter.

Mama smirked as she stared at her gorgeous daughter "You heard me gal what's going on?" she drawled in her deep southern accent.

"Mama, I slipped up and allowed another gal to come around Chio and he slept with her. She even had on the clothes he bought me," whined Daisy her fury returning.

"You did whaaaaat? Gal, you done lost ya fool-ass mind. That's rule number one. Never tell another beech about your sex. And don't have any huzzies all up in ya man's face, 'specially no pretty gal. You should be the only star shining in his eyes. Was she pretty?" asked Mama.

"She's a Spanish whore," Daisy said with jealousy covering her like a blanket. She had to admit to herself that Kitty was drop dead gorgeous but she would never say it out loud. Mama Jones stared at her daughter with pity, she knew Daisy was hurting knowing the other girl was Spanish was enough for Mama to know how the story ended.

"Gal, those Puerto Ricans are freaks. It's no telling what nastiness she done did to your man. Why on earth would you let her anywhere near Chio?" Mama asked not waiting for an answer. "As rich as that nigga is I wouldn't let his own mama near him."

Daisy curled up tighter wishing her mother would leave she wasn't feeling up to her lectures, she needed comfort and of course wasn't going to get it from her mother. Daisy learned from a baby that her mama didn't like to be hugged or kissed. She didn't show her children affection in the usual maternal fashion, her idea of motherly love was a good lecture. Before Daisy learned to talk she had to listen to her mama's condescending words of wisdom. She would say things like "crying ain't gonna get you nowhere in life, if you're hungry crawl your tail over here and get this here bottle."

Sure enough, Daisy learned to crawl at six months and was walking by eight months. Mama Jones purposely made her grow up fast. She schooled her in every aspect of life as she knew it to be. The only problem was that mama had a warped view of life. She taught her to use men and what they had to offer, instead of being independent and getting her own. She wanted Daisy to always be cared for so she didn't have to struggle like mama did with six children.

Mama Jones sat beside Daisy. She wanted to put her arms around her but didn't know how to perform a gesture as simple as that. So she patted Daisy's leg instead and told her to suck it up. "Stop feeling sorry for yourself gal and fight for your man."

"Mama I did. He smacked me and put me out of his club," whimpered Daisy. She left out the spitting part because it hurt her too badly to say it. She had never experienced that type of disrespect and couldn't deal.

"He threw you out of his club? This shit is serious." Mama yelled in disgust. She knew Chio was done with her if he was dissing her in that manner.

"Guess that means you're coming home ain't it?" Mama was disappointed and sad for her daughter. She knew the perks of her relationship with the rap star was about to be over. "You're beautiful Daisy. It's his loss you will always have a home to come back to." Daisy smiled—that was the nicest thing her mother had ever said to her, she started feeling better.

"Thanks, mama," she said

"Girl its plenty of rich men out there. You will score another big fish soon. Don't you worry, Doll Baby." Mama called her by her pet name and finished her pep talk with an uncustomary peck on Daisy's cheek.

Daisy glanced up shocked at her mother's unusual display of affection which she had to admit it felt good. She knew her mother loved her but she needed to feel it sometimes. Mama Jones always managed to put the energizer battery back in her back. She was recharged and ready to move on. Mama Jones hit the nail on the head when she said it's plenty of big fish in the sea. Fuck Chio. She needed to go fishing in a bigger sea. She decided to pay her cousin Kisha a visit. She lived in New York and knew everybody who was anybody. Daisy curled up under her blanket and dozed off dreaming about swimming in an ocean full of whales, she was a mermaid and the whales worshipped her, of course, she married the biggest fish in the sea.

CHAPTER 15

"Ooh, baby, right there…yessss…yess…lick it slow—thata girl…damn, ma, Super Head ain't got shit on you…yeah right there…that's it I'm cumming…oooh yesssssssss."

Mafia rolled over damn near suffocating the girl between her legs.

"Girl let my clit go, I can't take that shit after I nut," she moaned playfully, mushing her latest freak in the face. Mafia met her at Felicia Dawson's birthday bash—she was a popular lesbian WNBA player. Mafia loved partying with Dawson, she always had the baddest freaks at her parties. Not that Mafia needed any help bagging a fly chick. She had lesbians and straight women throwing their panties at her. She was an attractive, sexy and aggressive woman that favored the rapper *DaBrat* with a touch of *Alicia Keys*—that tomboy swagger with feminine sex appeal. Her body was as voluptuous as her cousin Daisy's and she drove both men and women crazy. She could have any man she wanted but she only desired women, although she didn't mind being seen with a notable *naire* every so often. Million or billion it didn't matter as long as he was a *naire*. That mindset was exactly why she was Daisy's favorite cousin.

Mafia was raised in New York but spent many summers in Atlanta visiting her family. She adored her Aunt Mama Jones and all her cousins, especially her younger cousin Daisy. She had her by fifteen years but Daisy was mature Mafia didn't mind having her around.

Mafia was currently involved in a relationship with a female *naire*. It was a well known yet unspoken secret—everybody in the music industry knew Mafia's girlfriend went both ways. She was an R&B superstar who was married to one of the most powerful moguls in the business. Diablo Black tolerated his wife's down low relationship and acted oblivious to her escapades with women because he had his own secrets. He had a penchant for running up in the tight hard ass of a homo thug every once in a while. He loved the roughneck thugs that ran through his record label. Gazelle, his wife and Mafia's lover would have killed him if she ever found out. She didn't think there was anything wrong with her affair with Mafia or her lust for women. She despised the homo-thugs that ran rampant throughout the music industry and would die if she ever discovered her own husband was down, she was a big hypocrite but didn't care she felt like two women were sexy and two men sucked.

Mafia sniffed a line of coke off of her latest freak's stomach when her phone rang. She fumbled around her nightstand hurriedly not wanting to miss the call she never knew if it was money or her honey Gazelle. Both were very important. She supplied all the *naires* in the music industry with the finest grade of cocaine. Whoever got high in the business usually copped from her. She flipped coke and ecstasy like pancakes. There were more drug addicts in the industry than in the hood with way more money to spend. She had workers posted at all the hot spots in New York, all the clubs were selling her products.

"Holla at ya girl?" she answered her phone with her usual sexy swagger.

"How's my favorite cousin doing up dere in that big ole apple?" purred Daisy.

"Hey, lil' cuz, what's crackin'? When am I gonna see you?" asked Mafia excitedly, she loved her baby cousin and wanted to show her off. She had a few *naires* she wanted to sic her on, first in line was Diablo Black. Mafia wanted him out of the picture. If he left Gazelle she could have her all to herself. She was madly in love with the superstar and wanted the world to know, she was tired of being her little secret. She admired celebrities like Ellen Degeneres that chose to live their lives openly without hiding the woman they loved. Mafia ignored the fact that not one openly gay celebrity was black. It was taboo for a black entertainer to admit being a homosexual. Mafia wanted Gazelle to be the one to kick the door open with her by her side, besides half the music industry was gay and afraid to come out for fear of losing their fans.

"Kisha, I need a break so I'mma come up and stay with you for a while."

"First of all you know I don't like being called Kisha, it's Mafia bighead," she scolded Daisy.

"Oh yeah I forgot Mafiaaaaa," drawled Daisy sarcastically.

"Aight no problem smart ass when is your' crazy ass coming?"

"ASAP." replied Daisy.

"Get ready to owe me big time," teased Mafia.

"Why?" squealed Daisy excitedly. "How does the richest *naire* in NY sound to you?" answered Mafia nonchalantly. Mafia grinned moving the phone from ear to ear trying to mute Daisy's happy squeals.

"Crazy, calm down. When you coming?"

"I'll be there tomorrow, I need this more than you know," said Daisy. Mafia suddenly sensed Daisy's sadness.

"Don't tell me my lil' cuz is fucked up over some dude."

"I'll tell you about it when I get there. I'm fittin' to book my flight now. I'll see you soon and Kish...I mean Mafia I love you," Daisy caught herself and called her cousin by the nickname she loved so much. She couldn't get used to her street name as much as she tried. Mafia was an OBG (Original Bad Girl) Daisy knew of her affiliation with the notorious clique and she knew Mafia was no joke, but to her, she was just her cool ass cousin Kisha from New York. She couldn't wait to see her. She needed the trip bad if there was anywhere that could cure Daisy's broken heart it was the big city.

CHAPTER 16

Mafia spotted Daisy as she stood by the baggage claim waiting for her luggage. *Damn*, she thought, *my baby cousin is sexy as hell.* She checked Daisy out from head to toe and she knew her plan would work. Diablo would love to have Daisy as his new arm candy, not only was she gorgeous, she was fly as hell. She was decked out in a pink bodysuit that fit her voluptuous curves like skin. She accessorized with her coveted pink purse that Anthony Davis bought her. She had her feet laced in her white Jacob the Jeweler customized diamond encrusted sneakers. She wore her curly hair loose so it framed her face sexily. She had on a touch of kissable couture lip gloss on her pouty lips and was absolutely stunning. Daisy Jones had arrived and everyone around her felt her presence.

"'Sup cuz you look bangin' baby girl, don't hurt nuttin' ma." Mafia grinned as she greeted her cousin beaming with pride as she twirled Daisy around checking her out.

"Thanks boo, you don't look too bad yourself" Daisy smiled giving her the once over. Mafia had her long hair braided into a cute design. She was clad in all black, simple yet sexy. She couldn't hide her sensuous physique in the wife beater and slim fit jeans she wore. She was far too pretty for the hardcore image she presented. Daisy was in awe of her cousin's beauty and couldn't figure out why she was so butch when she was so hot. Be that as it may, she loved and accepted her dear cousin for who she was but didn't feel the need to tell her about her own attraction to women. She didn't feel gay and certainly wasn't going to label herself because she enjoyed a good romp in the bed with her best friend every so often.

"Come on I have my driver waiting in the parking lot," Mafia said, grabbing Daisy's pink luggage set and escorted her to her truck. When she got her settled in her black Range Rover, she nestled down in the plush leather seat in the back of her truck and rolled a blunt. Daisy got comfy and nestled next to her, impressed with Mafia's chauffeur-driven Range.

"Cuz, what's up with this Hollywood shit? You got a damn female driver. Now that's a bitch ballin' out fo' sho,'" laughed Daisy.

"Yeah ma, I got to, I ain't stupid like those assholes driving around drunk and high. I lay back and chill and do me and sometimes do other things too," Mafia grinned and winked devilishly.

"Beech you crazy. I miss your nutty ass. Ooh, I'm gonna have so much fun with you," Daisy shouted gleefully. She needed a break from Atlanta, and being with her cousin in New York was just what the doctor ordered.

"Now what happened? What's the real reason you split town?" prodded Mafia. Daisy exhaled deeply and recounted the tale of her first broken heart. By the time she finished the story Mafia was in tears from laughing so hard. "You got that nigga back good girl, you spent seventy grand of his money and cracked his bitch in the head? Shit, I say you broke his heart. Forget him I got somebody that makes Young Chio look like young change," Mafia told Daisy all about Diablo Black omitting the part about being in love with his wife. She wanted to keep that part private for the moment until it was necessary to fill Daisy in. "So he's having a big birthday bash in a few weeks. Everybody will be there. Rihanna and Lady GaGa will be performing it's gonna be crazy and I want you to seduce him like only you can. You will meet him at Gazelle's record release party."

"Girl, you already know. I'm gonna make that nigga mine." Daisy beamed confidently, and Mafia grinned widely.

"That's what I'm talking about," she said, leaning back and daydreamed about her future wife, Gazelle. Everything was going to work itself out. Soon she would belong to her. She could count on Daisy to make it happen.

CHAPTER 17

"What do you mean the bitch left town?" Ivy said into the phone.

"I just spoke to her friend Anjel and she told me Daisy went to visit her cousin in New York," Coco stated calmly. "Yo the main thing is not to panic, I'll find out where she's staying and you can fly up there take care of your business and be back to collect your money within twenty-four hours—it's nothing – relax."

"That sounds simple just make it happen," ordered Ivy

Coco had succeeded in calming her nerves before Ivy spazzed out. She promised Chio she would take care of Daisy and she liked to keep her word. New York didn't sound like a bad idea, she needed a vacation and she stayed home sick. It wasn't anything like her hometown: the city that never slept. She would have to lay low but that wouldn't be a problem. She heard that the family of the dude she killed put a hit out on her, but the police had closed the case due to lack of evidence. She wasn't concerned about the hit. She knew her partner would make sure she was well protected. Mafia had New York on lock. She and Ivy were thick as thieves—they started the Original Bad Girls when they were wild young girls living in Fort Greene projects in Brooklyn.

The original crew was Ivy, Mafia, and Mistress. Ivy started a faction in Atlanta. Mafia had New York on lock. Mistress ran shit in prison. She was doing a five-year bid. They were the founders of the infamous OBG's. Ivy could always count on her girls to have her back. In the streets or behind the walls she had her OBG's. They were all over, ready to get paid or put in work. Ivy smoked a blunt and reminisced about one of their crazy escapades back in the days. They were in Fort Greene, a notorious housing projects in Brooklyn. The Fort had the highest murder rate of any projects at that time. Between that, the drug-related crimes, and the OBG's antics the PJs were off the chain. The girls were little badasses who grew up way to fast. Mafia was the only one out of the crew who had both parents, and by all accounts shouldn't have been running wild in the hood. The allure of street life made her defy her parents. Her family became her OBG's.

She met Ivy and Mistress in grade school. Mistress was the ringleader and usually came up with the schemes to get the money and fly gear the girls craved. "Eh, I got an idea to get us some minks," said Mistress. She was excited at the prospect of styling in a thirty thousand dollar full-length mink coat. She had been dreaming about how they were going to steal the expensive fur coats. They stole Guess, Polo, Tommy Hilfiger and every type of leather coat; but, fur coats were the big leagues. She had a plan and they were about to get paid.

"Mink coats. Say word. I'm feigning for a mink," Ivy said, almost choking on the joint they shared.

"Bitch,—puff, puff – pass," clowned Mafia mimicking her favorite comedian Chris Tucker's line from their favorite movie *Friday*. "Chill out, y'all. This shit is real if we do this right we'll have a couple of minks a piece plus mad furs to sell," Mistress said. She calculated the money the high-end coats would bring them—at least ten thousand apiece. She had a fence who bought all their merchandise for half price off the ticket price. At fourteen the girls should have been in the house studying for exams yet they were plotting a fur heist. "We're gonna need like ten more chicks to pull this one off" stated Mistress. "Alright I'll gather up the girls, where are we gonna meet?" asked Ivy her adrenaline was pumping anticipating the adventure. Mistress was deep in thought and didn't hear Ivy "Mistressss, we await your orders," yelled Ivy sarcastically. She was a bit envious of Mistress's position as leader but truthfully Mistress was the smartest one in the crew. She was the thinker. Ivy and Mafia were the enforcers they were always ready to bang out at a moment's notice. Mafia was a tomboy and could beat most of the boys in their school. Ivy was devious and would go as far as dropping rat poison in somebody's drink if they messed with her just on g.p (general purpose) thus the name Poison Ivy.

Mistress was indeed the brain in the organization. She had the connects' and handled the business side of their hustle. When they bought drugs to flip it was her connect they copped from. She knew all the hot boys in the hood. She taught the girls how to use stolen credit cards, picket pockets and boost. So she was the boss. She was a natural born leader and very grown for her young age.

She had an affair with an older married man who took care of her, so the girls started calling her Mistress. She came up with the idea to call their crew OBG's. She decided since the rapper Lil' Kim promoted herself as a bad girl, that they would call themselves Original Bad Girls. It was no question that they were true to the game and bad ass females in every way. The things she was rapping about they were doing in real life, well with the exception of "drinking babies," as her raunchy raps suggested.

Needless to say, the OBG's pulled off a legendary heist in midtown Manhattan. The newspapers reported a mob of unidentified females burglarized a midtown furrier. They got away with a quarter of a million dollars, worth of chinchillas, sables, and mink coats. When the police arrived they found the merchants bound and gagged in the fur vault in the back of his store. They were calling the girls the midtown fur bandits. There were no leads and no one was apprehended.

Ivy chuckled, missing the good old days badly. The early 80's was when hustling was at its prime and everybody was getting paid. It was nothing like those good old days. *Yeah*, she thought it would be good to visit her old stomping grounds. Mafia would be surprised and she would use her fake I.d to visit Mistress. She would take care of Daisy and stay for a few weeks and let Geechi miss her. She was ecstatic and high off the chronic she puffed, she felt great. She was the infamous Poison Ivy and she would soon be reunited with her girls OBG's for life. Ivy started packing for her trip.

CHAPTER 18

Gazelle squinted her eyes and focused on the bar in the crowded club. She could have sworn she spotted her woman flirting with another chick. The 40/40 club was packed with celebrities. Jay-Z threw the bash in her honor and her husband Diablo bought out the bar. Her table was littered with buckets of fine champagne and all her friends were there to help her celebrate her newest album. Her single was number one on the Billboard charts signaling multiplatinum success for her record. She was a megastar and loved being on top. She was the newest face for Cover Girl and her fragrance sold well. Gazelle loved being rich and famous and married to a powerful industry mogul. The world was hers and she was on the prowl. She wanted Mafia and whoever the pretty thang was that occupied all her time by the bar. Gazelle was far from jealous, she just wanted in on the fun. She was a super freak and loved her some girls. She was worst than a man. She had a harem of women at her disposal. She had to be discreet about her preference, after all, she was Diablo Black's wife. She did a good job hiding her desires and then she met Mafia.

Gazelle was at her loft in Tribeca lower Manhattan and she felt like scoring some coke to get high. She usually had Diablo supply her with her treats but she didn't want him to know about her 'bat cave', as she affectionately called the loft. So calling him was out of the question. A girl had to have her privacy. She liked to come to the loft when she needed to relax and freak off. She loved her husband, but sexually he couldn't please her. She needed the soft sensual touch of a woman to bring her to the heights of ecstasy that she craved. She only experienced orgasms with females. She loved the hard muscular body of a well-built man and the power and protection her husband afforded her, but that was about it, she hadn't found a man that would take her all the way there.

When a friend sent Mafia over to her loft to service her, Gazelle got more than the powder she loved to snort—she fell instantly in lust. Mafia locked eyes with Gazelle hypnotizing her with her lusty gaze. Gazelle's juices flowed as she let the pretty honey colored girl into her place.

"You have very beautiful eyes," Gazelle said, complimenting Mafia on her almond shaped dark brown eyes.

"Thanks, you're hot too, ma. Your magazine covers don't show this side of you. I like it." Mafia whispered in her ear seductively returning the compliment. She stood so close to her that Gazelle felt her tits harden as they grazed her arm. She blushed at the compliment and smiled coyly. She knew she was pretty, but Mafia made her feel gorgeous. Gazelle had a deep dark brown completion and when she wasn't performing she wore her hair natural in a curly short fro, her lips were full and heart-shaped and her teeth were sparkling white and perfect. She was an amazing looking woman even without the makeup and wigs she usually wore. She flicked her tongue seductively and smiled her million dollar smile.

"Have a seat, sexy. Where are my goodies?" Gazelle asked as she grabbed Mafia's hand and led her to her plush velvet sectional. Gazelle was unusually nervous although she didn't show it. She was taken back by Mafia's oblivion to her star status. She didn't seem starstruck or intimidated by Gazelle like most people were. Her nonchalant swagger turned her on.

"It depends on what type of goodies you want from me?" Mafia flirted as she stretched out quite comfortably on the super star's couch. She made herself at home and it drove Gazelle crazy with lust. She could hardly control herself. Mafia wore her trademark black wife beater with no bra. Her 34b's stood perky and her nipples were pointy beckoning Gazelle to suck her hard nipples. Her stomach was washboard flat and her hips swelled in her tight black leather biker pants. She had her black Ed Hardy helmet resting beside her and square-toed boots stretched out on the couch. She was the hottest biker chick Gazelle had ever seen. She wanted to lean over and lick the parts between the braided designs in her head. She was in pure freak mode.

"I want both of your goodies so I can see which one taste better," she purred as she opened the ounce of raw cocaine Mafia handed her and rubbed the pearly flakes on her gums. Her mouth numbed instantly and the only flavor she wanted to taste was Mafia. She leaned in slowly and pulled the sexy drug dealer by her studded dog collar and kissed her lips softly. Passion overcame her as heat surged thru her loins. She stood up abruptly pulling Mafia gently to her freak chamber. The room was midnight black with a mirrored wall traveling the length of the custom-made room. The cathedral ceilings in the spacious loft made the dark space cavernous. Candles flickered eerily, glowing over the whips, chains and sex toys hanging from the walls and a steel encased king sized bed which stood majestically in the center of the floor. Mafia glanced around until her eyes rested on the swing that hung from the wall and the mechanical bull with the large black dildo protruding from its seat. She was stunned and immensely turned on. The seemingly demure singer was a masochistic freak and Mafia loved it. Suffice to say the two became lovers instantly.

Gazelle loved Mafia but she needed more than one woman to satisfy her carnal desires. After two years together she made Mafia her main lover and was careful when she cheated on her. Mafia was crazy about her and insanely jealous. She was even jealous of her husband, which baffled Gazelle because she had no intentions of leaving him and besides it was plenty of her to go around. She chuckled and stroked her pussy under the table as she recalled their first encounter.

Gazelle stood gracefully, adjusting her mini Zac Posen gown and glided thru the throng of well-wishers to greet her woman. Mafia's heartbeat quickened when she saw Gazelle approaching her thru the crowd. She felt the familiar stirrings of lust butterfly through her stomach she was mesmerized by her African goddess. Gazelle's parents were from Nigeria, Africa, and she carried herself like an African queen. Mafia admired Gazelle's high cheekbones and exotic cat shaped eyes. She loved her natural beauty and also appreciated the glamorous side of her. She had on a jet black waist length wig with sharp Chinese bangs. Gazelle was any man's desire and Mafia was honored to be the woman in her life. She would do anything to have her all to herself.

"Hey, gorgeous congratulations." Mafia greeted her lover affectionately.

"Thanks, baby. Are you enjoying yourself?" inquired Gazelle as she checked Daisy out. She stared pointedly waiting for an introduction.

"Yes, we are. Gazelle this is my cousin Daisy. She's visiting from Atlanta." Mafia introduced the two beautiful women.

"Oh, that's nice. Hello, Daisy, you look lovely. I hope Mafia is showing you a good time?" Gazelle smiled, putting Daisy at ease.

"Thank you. I'm a big fan of yours and my cousin is showing me a terrific time," said Daisy. She couldn't believe how cool her cousin was with the superstar.

"Why don't you bring Daisy to the Hamptons this weekend, we'll do a girls retreat. It will be the last time I'll be able to relax before my international tour begins," Gazelle smiled invitingly. She wanted to spend time with Mafia before she left and wouldn't mind sampling a piece of Miss Daisy. Gazelle smiled slyly at the southern bombshell. She knew Mafia would never suspect her ulterior motive for the retreat or her attraction for her cousin. She didn't know if Daisy was into females and really didn't care, Gazelle always got what she wanted and she wanted Daisy.

Mafia would die if she knew what Gazelle was up to. She didn't have a clue how freaky Gazelle actually was, she didn't realize she cheated on her. Gazelle had sex with damn near every bisexual or straight up lesbian in the industry. She had an insatiable appetite for women from the female record executives to the dancers in her videos. She turned females out right and left. It wasn't hard. She discovered the freak in every woman. Once she piqued their curiosity, getting them into her freak chambers was easy. She knew about Mafia's sideline hoe's and Diablo's mistress's so she did her thing as well. It was not fair if she didn't get her shit off like everyone else.

What she didn't know is that Diablo played with men too his down low tendencies were a well-guarded secret. If she ever got a whiff of the atrocity she would have killed him. She hated butch men together in a relationship. Soft boys were one thing. She had plenty of gay male friends: her makeup artist, background singers, and dancers. She had absolutely no patience for homo thugs—they disgusted her and they ran wild throughout the industry.

Women were another story she loved them, especially pretty young things like Mafia's cousin. Daisy was so happy to be included in the trip to the Hamptons that she could have hugged Gazelle.

"That sounds fun. I can't wait," she squealed.

"I can't wait either." Mafia grinned sexily at Gazelle.

"Alright, then it's a date. Oh, there goes Diablo. Let me go, Mafia, call me later hon," said Gazelle as she glided off to greet her husband. Mafia caught an instant attitude. Daisy picked up on the 'tude and put two and two together.

"OMG, your sleeping with ole girl, ain't ya?" She already knew the answer, because she knew her cousin and sensed the sexual vibes between her and Gazelle.

"You already know how big cuz get down," bragged Mafia. "Listen, remember the naire, I told you about?"

"Yeah, where is he? I'm ready for his ass." Daisy smoothed her hands along the contours of her voluptuous body. She was ready to put her sexiest game down on Diablo Black.

"Oh snap," she gasped as she realized that Diablo was the same name Gazelle had just mentioned. "Is she fucking with him?" she asked Mafia.

"Yeah, that's her husband" stated Mafia blandly as she guided Daisy from the bar so they could talk privately. "I'm going to distract Gazelle while you go introduce yourself to Diablo. Once he sees you he'll be all over you. Get his number and pretend you have to leave. I don't want Gazelle to see you talking to him. OK?"

"No problem cuz I'm on it. He's a cutie pie, too, that's a plus. kind of big for my taste but as long as his paper is just as large I'm good." schemed Daisy. "You want me to take him from Gazelle huh?"

"Yeah you got that right on the head," Mafia replied smugly "I want that nigga OUT of the picture."

"You're in love with her ain't ya?" teased Daisy

"I want her all to myself and I'm willing to do whatever, to make it happen," Mafia replied darkly. Daisy realized Mafia was dead serious, she saw murder in her eyes. Gazelle was her drug and she had her strung out. She couldn't get enough of her and she hated sharing her. "Oh before I forget don't sleep with him the word is out that he's on some down low fag shit," warned Mafia.

"Damn. Say it ain't so as grisly and cute as he is. Wow don't worry, even if he's not dipping I'm not giving up my goldmine, it's still untapped," stated Daisy proudly.

"That's what's up ma—you still holding out. I'm impressed and I'm proud of you, lil' cuz that's what the fuck I'm talking about.

"I'm a virgin, too." confided Mafia. "I've never slept with a man. Got me some blazing head but never went all the way, a girl popped my cherry."

"How the hell did a girl pop your cherry?" Daisy asked amazed at her cousin's confession.

"Same way a nigga could have. Only she used a plastic dick. That motherfucker felt real as hell." Mafia smiled as she remembered the first girl who ever used a strapped on a dildo to fuck her. She was a stud, a very aggressive girl who looked so masculine she could have easily passed for a boy. Mafia was fifteen years old and couldn't decide if she was into boys or girls. The stud had Mafia curious with her hardcore style and lured her into her bed after unusual circumstances. Mafia was a tomboy and used to kick ass in sports, she played ball like a dude and used to tear up the courts in her housing projects.

One afternoon she was slinging nickels of crack in front of her building when BoyBoy came up to her. The stud was appropriately called BoyBoy. "What's up Kisha wanna play some one on one?" she asked her.

"First of all didn't I tell you not to call me by my government name? My name is Mafia to you," she growled, annoyed at the stud for making her feel butterflies in her stomach for some reason she couldn't explain. She had a secret crush on BoyBoy and was mad at herself because she didn't want to feel those feelings for a girl. BoyBoy was eighteen and proud of her sexuality. The boys in their hood accepted her lifestyle and considered her one of the 'boys'. It might have been for the fact that she had eight brothers who would have put a bullet in anyone that dared to disrespect their lesbian sister.

"Come on, Shorty, you don't know nuttin' 'bout being in da mafia. What makes you a gangsta? You and your lil' bullshit crew jumping bitches?" BoyBoy snickered purposely trying to get under Mafia's skin.

"Naw, I'm gangsta' cuz I fuck dyke bitches like you up," Mafia said, punching the stud in her stomach.

Mafia caused her to double over in excruciating pain. She pummeled her with lightning-quick blows until she wore herself out. Mafia slumped down next to BoyBoy's crumpled body, panting for breath. The stud was astonished at the ferocity of Mafia's blows and impressed with the beating. Boyboy couldn't believe, she whooped her ass like that.

"Bitch you crazy," BoyBoy gasped. Mafia lunged at her and grabbed her by the throat. "What's my name?" she demanded.

BoyBoy wiped the blood from her busted lip and wheezed "Mafia" as she gasped for air. Mafia jumped up and pulled the stud off the ground and dragged her into the building. BoyBoy was grateful no one was around to witness the humiliating beat down. Mafia felt bad so she took her upstairs to her apartment to clean the wounds. Her parents were at work so she wouldn't get into trouble. They hated when she fought the boys or in this case the dykes in the projects.

While Mafia cleaned BoyBoy's busted lip with peroxide the strangest feeling came over her, she had an uncontrollable urge to kiss her bruised lips. Their eyes locked and before she knew it BoyBoy had her jeans down and her head between Mafia's legs. She ate her out until she begged her to stop, Mafia had never felt such pleasure and what she felt next almost made her pass out. BoyBoy had on a strap-on dildo and slipped it inside of her with the deftness of a seasoned lover. She didn't miss a stroke and was gentle enough not to hurt Mafia while taking her virginity. The stud turned Mafia all the way out, she had become a straight up lesbian. It was a day she would never forget and the beginning of many sexual trysts between the two rivals although it ended shortly when Mafia beat the stud down for cheating on her. She shook her head and laughed as the memories came and went. She was far removed from the sexually inexperienced teenager she used to be. "Anyway cuz, I want you to Daisytize that chump and get him outta my way."

I gotcha, oooh, lemme make my move now.

Gazelle walked away. Daisy spotted Diablo sitting by himself and strutted over to him. The game had just begun. Mafia went to find Gazelle. She needed to feel her soft lips against hers. She loved fooling around right under Diablo's nose. Soon she would be free to be with her girl openly and if Daisy couldn't work her magic, Mafia would have to work hers and make Diablo disappear. Mafia smiled devilishly as she went off in search of the love of her life.

CHAPTER 19

Ivy arrived in New York energetic and ready to visit all her favorite stores. She loved to shop and had fifty pieces of plastic (credit cards) to work with. Her connects supplied her with all the personal information she would need to make withdrawals from the accounts, so she was straight. She charged a suite at the Four Seasons, one of the five-star hotels in Manhattan. She registered under the assumed identity, Margaret Von Baron. Ivy laughed at how easy it was to become someone else, with the right credentials she had easily become a rich forty-year-old woman. She dressed up for her role wearing her hair in an elegant chignon and she covered her eyes with a pair of bug-eyed vintage Chanel shades for the benefit of the security cameras. She wore a dazzling diamond choker around her neck and a five-carat diamond ring. She looked every bit the part of a well-bred millionaire.

Race wasn't an issue. She had the driver license altered with the information she supplied, as long as the name and date of birth matched she was straight. The bellhop unpacked her luggage set and left her to enjoy the lavish suite. "I'm that Bitch.", Ivy said to herself, she felt like she was on top of the world living a life people only dreamed of and it was all built on a con. The reality was it would all be over if she made one wrong move. She was one of the best hustlers in the game so she rarely worried about getting caught. She planned to do some personal shopping and hit some electronic stores. She had an order for fifty laptops which would bring her close to seventy-five hundred dollars after liquidation. The money that she was going to collect from Chio for the hit would be for her play money. She would use it to treat herself at the spa. Ivy lived like a celebrity that was what being an OBG was all about.

She decided to call Mafia once she settled in she was so excited to be back in town and couldn't wait to see her old running partner. After an exhausting day of shopping on 5th Avenue, Ivy spent thousands at Gucci, Chanel and her favorite department store Saks Fifth Avenue. She ordered room service and settled down to call Mafia. She dialed her cell and didn't recognize the voice that answered the phone. "Hello, Mafia?"

"No this is her cousin she sleep right now can I take a message?" answered Daisy.

"Yeah tell her to call this number back. I'm trying to surprise her so I won't leave my name," replied Ivy.

"Well, Hunny, that might not work. Mafia is very busy, so tell me your name. If it's important she'll get back to you," replied Daisy with an attitude. Ivy was caught off guard and almost stuttered at the audacity of the bitch that had just checked her.

"Listen, this is Ivy she'll get back to me. Matter fact what's your name?" Ivy countered throwing shade right back at her.

"Daisy, I'll tell her you called if I remember," click. Daisy hung the phone up rudely. She didn't like the girl's attitude and thought she was probably one of Mafia's jump offs. She scribbled a note with her name and stuck it on the fridge. She was annoyed by the rude attitudes the New Yorkers seem to be born with. She wasn't going to let it spoil her day. She was excited because Diablo invited her to his Recording Studio. Everything went as planned at the party and he called her the next day and told her he wanted to record her in his studio. For some reason, he wanted to hear her sing. He kept raving about how beautiful she was and how he would make her a star. Daisy felt great. She loved his compliments. It was just what she needed to boost her self-esteem after the whole Chio fiasco. She knew she would have Diablo wrapped around her finger in no time.

Meanwhile, Ivy was sitting on her bed dumbfounded staring at her phone in shock. Did that country bitch just say her name was Daisy? The voice had a southern accent, although very professional, she didn't sound ghetto but it just might be "the" Daisy. Ivy couldn't believe her luck and had to confirm if the sassy hoe on the phone was indeed the chick, she came to New York to rip apart. She called CoCo's cell. She knew she would be able to give her the juicy juice on Daisy's whereabouts. "Eh, yo, CoCo where is that chick Daisy Jones staying at up here?" Asked Ivy.

"Well hello to you, too. Damn you so rude, yo," CoCo shot back annoyed at being interrupted by Ivy. She was taking a rare moment to study for a test.

"Yeah, yeah whatever I'm up here and I need info on ole girl, cuz, I'm buggin'. I just called Mafia and some country bitch answered her jack and said she was her cousin Daisy. Please tell me it ain't the same chick," grumbled Ivy. She was irate at the stupid coincidence. She knew she shouldn't even consider violating Mafia's cousin, but the griminess in her wouldn't let her back down. She simply had no morals, no code of honor, nothing. As long as it was beneficial for her she would risk crossing her partner for no reason but the thrill of it. Ivy was a cold-hearted bitch and she didn't know how to be any other way. Poison seeped out of her.

"Oh shit, hold on lemme three-way Anjel and find out exactly where she's at." CoCo clicked off the line and dialed Anjel's number. She clicked back and quickly told Ivy not to speak as Anjel's phone rang.

"What's up girl?" answered Anjel cheerily.

"Nothing much, where's Daisy staying in New York? I'm going up for the weekend and I want to get up with her," CoCo lied glibly.

"I just spoke to her she's in Harlem with her cousin."

"Oh, what's her cousin name? I might know her."

"Her name is Kisha but they call her Mafia," Anjel happily answered, not realizing she was being played."

"Oh snap. That's my Homie. She's legendary in my hood. She's from Brooklyn. She's a thorough ass broad. I'm going to definitely holla at them when I get up top," said CoCo.

"Good. Daisy will love to see you. Is Casey going with you?"

"Naw I'm gonna make a quick trip, I gotta take care of something. I'm going to surprise them so don't let Daisy know I'm coming."

"OK, have fun. I'll be up there soon too. It's a big party going down for Diablo Black and Daisy invited me," bragged Anjel.

"Shit, Daisy moves fast, I forgot Mafia is well connected in the industry. Them bitches are having a ball. I can't wait to get there," said CoCo. No longer running game, she decided she would really pay Daisy a visit since she figured the hit was off now that Ivy knew for sure Daisy was Mafia's cousin. Nobody in their right mind would fuck with Mafia's people, especially since they all 'repped OBG hard. That would be a definite violation.

The twins grew up admiring Ivy, Mafia, and Mistress. They were beside themselves with joy when they hooked up with Ivy, in Atlanta and became certified OBG's. They ran into her in the Lenox mall when they first arrived in Atlanta and they clicked instantly. She put them down on her team and they have been getting money together ever since. The twins had idolized the OBG's for years and weren't going to turn down an opportunity to belong to the notorious money getting clique for nothing even if it meant paying dues to Ivy. It was worth it, just to be known as an Original Bad Girl, there was no higher honor in the hustling world. They were some bad ass money getting chicks who didn't hesitate to bust their guns and bring it to a sucker's ass. CoCo said goodbye to Anjel and made sure she clicked her off the line before she resumed talking to Ivy. "Ain't that a bitch. This is a small damn world. Oh well, I guess Chio gonna have to give homegirl a pass," CoCo said to Ivy.

"Why would he do that?" Ivy asked her nonchalantly.

"Uh....cuz she's Mafia cousin and that makes her untouchable, doesn't it?" stammered CoCo flabbergasted at Ivy's tone of voice. If she didn't know better she would have thought she still wanted to go thru with it.

"A hit is a hit point blank. The bitch still gotta get it. I gave Chio my word."

"But Mafia is your partner. How could you cross her for Chio? That's some foul shit Ivy," lectured CoCo disgustingly.

"Bitch please it ain't like I'm going to do anything to Mafia. Plus the bitch Daisy got smart with me on the horn," Ivy returned snottily knowing damn well what she was saying didn't justify the trifling shit she wanted to do. She had no loyalty to anyone and in her own twisted mind, she didn't understand that she was wrong. "Come on CoCo, it's a job, it's just business. Don't get all melodramatic about it," said Ivy.

"What happened to the codes we suppose to live by? Death before dishonor. Never flip over dick. You taught us that," CoCo ranted hysterically. "You told us never snitch. Never let a nigga come between us. And never flip on each other. We're supposed to be family. OBG for life. I got it tatted on my arm," said CoCo, trying to talk some sense into Ivy.

"I'm not flipping on Mafia, I'm flipping on her country ass cousin. I don't know that broad and I don't owe her anything. She ain't down with OBG. Now are you with me or against me?" Ivy asked stonily, "Or are you going to cross me for dat bitch?" asked Ivy.

CoCo paused for a minute to contemplate the situation. She didn't want beef with Ivy and Daisy did cross her cousin Anthony. She sighed, defeated. "I'm with you. You're right. Fuck da hoe. Just don't let Mafia find out cuz I'm not trying to go at it with her over this shit," CoCo warned her.

"Don't worry she'll never know get your ass up here I'm staying at the Four Seasons and its fly as hell you can crash in my suite. I'll charge you a plane ticket tomorrow," Ivy said excitedly.

"OK, but I can't leave until this weekend," replied CoCo.

"No problem. I have this suite for two weeks, I got plenty of work for us we're going to have a ball tearing up the stores then I'll tear up Daisy," cackled Ivy, laughing at her own joke. CoCo cringed inwardly, she realized Ivy was ruthless and she didn't like it but she didn't have enough nerve to go against her. She only hoped Mafia didn't find out. She never actually hung out with her but her reputation preceded her she wasn't called Mafia for anything.

CoCo remembered hearing how Mafia tortured a guy for trying to rape her. They found dude's penis swinging from a street pole in Fort Greene. She didn't fuck around "Aight girl I'll see you soon," CoCo clicked Ivy off and finished studying.

Ivy nestled comfortably in between the 600 thread count Egyptian cotton sheets on the swanky hotel bed plotting on Daisy's fate. She was about to call Mafia when her cell rang in her hand. She looked at her caller I.D. and smiled. "What's up Mafia, I was just sitting here thinking about you girl."

"My motherfucking bitch Poison Ivy what's crackin' ma?" Mafia laughed happy to hear from her old partner in crime.

"Nothing, I'm home and you know I had to check in. I miss you Mafia," Ivy squealed.

"I miss you too baby girl. When am I going to see you? Where are you staying?"

"I'm at the Four Seasons. I'll be here for a minute. Let's do dinner tonight. How 'bout Sylvia's?" Ivy offered referring to the popular soul food restaurant in Harlem.

"Hell yeah, I'm feigning for her collard greens and mac and cheese. Yo, I'ma bring my cousin wit' me, she's from ATL you might know her."

"Yeah, what's her name?" asked Ivy nonchalantly.

"Daisy Jones. She was getting them niggas down there, she's a bad bitch you'll love her," Mafia bragged proudly. "Naw, I never heard of her. It's so many females running around

Atlanta, it's hard to keep track. Only New Yorkers stick out. We're the outsiders, but now that I think of it, I think she buys shit from my workers. The twins always talk about a Daisy, who spends gees with them," Ivy lied glibly

"Yup, that's gotta be my cuz. She stays fly, any way you'll meet her tonight, what time?"

"I'll be there by nine o'clock. I just gotta jump in the shower, I've been shopping all day," yawned Ivy.

"I know you have bitch. I know how you get down. Bring ya girl something cute. I know you done robbed Fifth Ave blind," chuckled Mafia, knowing how greedy Ivy was.

"I got you, Mafia. I got a couple of Louis Vuitton wallets and a Fendi coat you might like."

"Sounds good I'll see you later," Mafia ended the call. The last time she saw Ivy was a couple of years ago right before she left dude stinking—dead—in Brooklyn. Ivy had been in the wind ever since. Mafia shook her head and laughed to herself as she thought about Poison Ivy and her antics. Ivy was her right-hand girl. When they were teenagers they ran around Brooklyn terrorizing shit.

Mafia would never forget the time they kidnapped a bitch for fucking Terror, Mistress's man. It was her, Ivy, Nelly Pop, Lil' Lisa and Asia. The girls were high as kites. Nelly Pop was a dust head and turned the girls on to some 'sherm' she had copped from uptown. Mistress was locked up in juvenile detention doing a twelve-month stretch. She found out her boyfriend, Terror was screwing around with this chick she was cool with named Tela so she called Mafia crying. That was all it took for the OBG's to bring it to Tela's ass. Mafia had Asia call Tela and pretended she wanted her to braid her hair. When she arrived at Asia's crib in the Pj's everything appeared normal until she finished Asia's hair. She had no idea they knew she was sleeping with Terror and was totally unprepared for what happened next.

The girls started teasing her and cracking jokes. At first, she thought they were playing until things got physical. Tela was a soft-spoken, petite, light skinned girl and way out of her league against the rough girls that harassed her. "Yo, this bitch think she all that," Mafia snarled when Tela asked Asia to pay her twenty dollars for the braids so she could leave. The girls were getting far too rowdy for her taste and she began feeling uneasy. She had a guilty conscience because she knew she was creeping with Mistress's man on the low and prayed her spot wouldn't get blown up. She slowly realized that she had fallen into their trap and it was too late.

"Stop playin', y'all. I just need my dough. But that's OK Asia, I'll get it later," said Tela nervously, walking to the door.

"You hear this nasty ho?" spat Mafia "She'll pay you later? No bitch you're gonna pay now for disrespecting my motherfucking homegirl" Tela froze as she digested Mafia's harsh words, her eyes darted wildly as the pack of wild teens advanced on her closing her inside of a tight circle. She knew then that the gig was up.

Nelly Pop raced her to the door on her heels as Tela tried to sprint to the door hoping to escape. "Uh ,uh, bitch" Nelly Pop pulled out her pearl handle .22 and stuck it in Tela's ear. "You must need me to blow the wax outta ya ear cuz you ain't listening. Sit your trifling ass down," giggled Nelly Pop evilly. She was tripping off the Sherm she smoked and found the whole situation hilarious. She wanted to pop Tela in her ear just to see if wax would pour out—instead of blood, she was trigger happy thus the name Nelly "POP"

"Chill, Nelly Pop. Let's have some fun first," ordered Mafia. "Bring that Bitch to the bathroom." Ivy and Asia sprang into action. They grabbed Tela's legs from under her and slammed her to the floor and dragged the terrified girl to the bathroom. Tela tried to kick and scream but Mafia bashed her in the head with a frying pan as they passed thru Asia's tiny kitchen. "Shut up bitch, can't nobody save your ass now you weren't screaming when you were fucking Mistress's man or was you?" Mafia joked and the girls broke out in delirious laughter. Tela was scared to death she had never been so scared in her life, she cried silently and tried to protect her face from getting lumped up from the pan. Blood trickled down her forehead leaking into her eyes. She prayed frantically pleading with God to spare her life. She knew the maniacs that held her captive were capable of anything. She only hoped to make it out alive, Terror's dick was not worth dying over. "Lil' Lisa bring me a rope and put the radio on" ordered Mafia. The girls piled up in Asia's small bathroom and dumped Tela in the tub. "Ivy pull her clothes off" commanded Mafia. Ivy complied ripping Tela's blouse, she tried to ply her jeans down but couldn't get them past the squirming girls hips. Ivy was high and appeared to be moving in slow motion. Tela took advantage of Ivy's slow movements and swiftly kicked her in her stomach a move that cost her dearly.

"No this bitch didn't kick me," yelped Ivy, staggering from the blow. She was fueled by anger and suddenly hopped on the edge of the tub and karate kicked Tela in the face. By the time she finished stomping the poor girl's face, her Timbs were covered in blood. Mafia took the rope from Lil' Lisa as she bopped her head to Eric B and Rakim's song, "*I ain't no joke*" and tied the brutally beaten semiconscious girl's hands together. Tela was spitting up blood and teeth.

"Pass me some alcohol and a blade Asia," barked Mafia. She was amped up and the sight of Tela's bloody face made her vicious nature surface. She turned into a beast, with no conscience and didn't feel the least bit sorry for the battered girl. She only wished Mistress could have been there to see the work they put in for her. She loved her childhood best friend and had no problem beating anyone's ass for her she knew she would do the same for her. They all would ride or die for each other they were OBG's for life.

When Asia passed Mafia the blade she slashed Tela across her chest carving an M on top of her breast. "Look y'all, I gave her an M for my girl Mistress, so when Terror go to suck her tits he can remember who he belongs to. Even though I doubt he's gonna want her anymore, this bitch ain't got no front teeth."

joked Mafia cruelly making the girls crack up at her insensitive humor. They stood around the tub in the cramped bathroom laughing hysterically. Mafia finally ended the brutal attack by dousing Tela with Alcohol, she splashed the burning liquid on her face and they watched as Tela writhed in agony. Tela screeched as the whelps and cuts on her body bubbled up with foam from the alcohol. Mafia remembered how vigilant she felt handling that situation for Mistress. That's what their clique was all about. Loyalty, one for all and all for one. She loved the OBG's especially Ivy and Mistress they all came up together and would always have each other's back. She knew she didn't have to ever worry about one of her girls crossing her. It was death before dishonor—or so she thought.

CHAPTER 20

Daisy instantly disliked her cousin's friend. She felt bad vibes from her, especially after their little phone spat. She wasn't feeling Ivy at all but she had to be cordial to her out of respect for Mafia. Daisy couldn't wait to leave the Sylvia's. She had a late night session with Diablo that she was anxious to get to. She was so excited at the prospect of making a record and hoped she could pull it off so she could show Young Chio that Kitty wasn't the only one with talent. Daisy knew if Diablo put his money behind her she could go far and blow Kitty out of the box. Not that she wanted Chio back because he had hurt her too badly. She just wanted to show him what he had lost. She would be bigger and better than Kitty could ever be in the industry. She was Daisy Mother-Fuckin' Jones and bad to the bone.

She said her goodbyes to Mafia and Ivy and caught a cab to Diablo's studio. Daisy loved Manhattan it was so alive, so much action at all times and its nickname *The City That Never Sleeps'* was perfect for the bustling city. The cab driver drove like a psychopath. Daisy felt like she was on a roller coaster ride as she bounced all over the passenger seat of the cab. The driver swerved wildly trying to avoid potholes the size of craters. She held on for dear life and as terrifying as the trip was she was thrilled and loved every bit of it.

When the Middle Eastern driver pulled up in front of the warehouse building in the Chelsea section of lower Manhattan he leered at Daisy and smiled a toothless grin. "You pay ten dollars and fifty cents pretty lady," he said, flirting in his broken English. He undressed Daisy with his perverted eyes as she paid the fair and hopped out the cab. She gave him an eye full as she sashayed to the building hypnotizing the horny cabbie with each switch of her heart-shaped ass. Daisy looked at the giant buildings lining the deserted industrial block and became nervous. She hurried into the building and was greeted by a man as huge as a refrigerator. She was relieved when he identified himself as Diablo's bodyguard. "You must be Daisy? Diablo's expecting you. Come with me." The mammoth bodyguard escorted Daisy to the elevator and she tingled with anticipation —she felt like she was in a movie, the whole scene was so elusive. When the doors opened to the enormous studio she gasped.

"Damn this is off da chain." she squealed making the stony bodyguard smiled. He was used to females reacting like that and envied his boss, knowing he was about to put it on the fine fat ass beauty. Diablo spared no expense on his studio. She walked on a beautiful plush monogrammed black carpet with white lettering that spelled out "Black Entertainment" and the company's logo. She stared up in awe at the black crystal chandelier towering above her head. The walls were covered in Italian black and white marble. He had a massive oversized black suede sectional with white fur blankets scattered haphazardly over the sofa. Daisy tensed up immediately when she spotted three scantily clad, beautiful women lounging on the sectional couch—they were playing video games and barely glanced at Daisy. She was led into a state of the art recording studio that resembled a NASA space station. Daisy stared at the high tech machines and the huge recording booth and became instantly intimidated. She was way out of her league and didn't want to make a fool out of herself. Diablo Black was the real deal. He made Young Chio look like a small time country bumpkin.

She did her research and Googled Diablo so she knew he wasn't the run of the mill rapper turned C.E.O., he was a corporate attorney who built his empire on various business ventures. When he met Gazelle he bought her out of her contract at Arista Records and secured a deal with Universal Records to start his own label Black Entertainment. She was the superstar on his label and Daisy was so flattered that he wanted to record her when he had such success with his wife. She would soon find out. "Hello, beautiful I'm glad you could make it" Diablo greeted her with a huge smile of approval on his face.

Daisy looked edible in her cherry red latex spandex that fitted her voluptuous body like a second skin. She was oozing with sex appeal as usual. She gained confidence when she saw the lust in his eyes that was a look she was all too familiar with and knew how to control. She felt better realizing that although he was powerful she still held her own power and she would use it to her advantage.

"I'm happy to be here Diablo. I hope I don't disappoint you because as I told you at the party, I am not an expert singer," Daisy said modestly.

"Don't you worry about that most of the singers in the game can't sing well live. It's all in the machines, baby. I have equipment that will make your voice sound like Mariah Carey's. It's your presence and your attitude that I'm interested in. You carry yourself like a star and you're beautiful. I think you are the sexiest chocolate sista, I've seen in a long time. All we need is a hit song and kaboom,"—he shouted kaboom, startling Daisy —"and you're a star. What do you think about that?"

"I know that's right. Let's get to work, Big Daddy," said Daisy sassily. Diablo burst out laughing he loved Daisy's down home southern personality. No one had ever called him big daddy he liked the nickname and couldn't wait to hear her scream it at the top of her lungs while he screwed her to death. He had big plans for Daisy he was grooming her to take over Gazelle's position as the first lady of Black Entertainment. He hated his wife and she had no idea how he really felt about her. He despised how she whored around with women. She thought he didn't know but there wasn't much Diablo didn't know about her. He was the laughing stock of the industry. Her behavior was despicable and it was part of the reason he slept with men occasionally.

He liked to use that as an excuse, but he knew he had always had an attraction to men ever since his uncle molested him when he was twelve. He was ashamed of his fetish but he loved to run up in a muscular ass every now and then. He would never stop loving women and needed a beautiful woman on his arms, Gazelle was an embarrassment and it was time to replace and upgrade her. Daisy was the perfect candidate. He took her into the recording booth and told her to sing whatever she knew the words to and felt comfortable singing. Daisy belted out her best rendition of Keyshia Cole's *Love*. Once Diablo's engineer programmed her voice in the computer and ran her vocals through the machine, he pressed a few buttons and in an hour she sounded better than Keyshia Cole. "I sound amazing. How is that possible? Oh my gawd, Diablo it's like magic," shrieked Daisy with joy. She couldn't believe how great she sounded.

"I told you, baby, you are a star." The wheels were in motion and Daisy's destiny was set. She wouldn't have to depend on another man's riches again. She was going to be rich and famous and Young Chio would regret ever dissing her for that whore Kitty. Daisy smiled dreamily and began recording her hit record.

CHAPTER 21

Everything happened extremely fast for Kitty—one minute she was recording one song and the next week she was completing an entire album. Chio named it Kitty Kat and he already had her first single blowing up the local radio stations in Atlanta. Kitty was a huge hit—she performed at all clubs and attended all the hot parties. She never went back to Magic's. Life couldn't get any better for Kitty if only she could get Daisy out of Chio's system completely. After the incident at his club, all Chio did was obsess about getting revenge on her. Kitty believed in her heart that he still had a thing for Daisy Jones and she didn't like it one bit. She tried everything to distract him, after all, she was the one with the stitches in her head and if she was willing to let it go why couldn't he? All the pain she suffered was worth getting Daisy out of the picture. She loved having Young Chio all to herself and she was determined to get her off of his mind.

Kitty sauntered into Chio's bedroom in a sexy red La Perla lace negligee' and crawled across his king size mattress seductively. Chio was sprawled out comfortably, puffing a blunt filled with Hurricane, a potent mixture of ganja and cocaine. He was zoned out and stared at the Spanish beauty through half closed glazed pupils. He stroked her long hair and petted her face. "Hey, Mami, what it do?" he said lazily. Kitty felt herself getting moist. She could never get enough of Chio's long thick penis inside of her.

"You know what it do Papi," she whispered, spreading her legs and climbed on top of him. She slipped his semi-hard cock inside of her and rode him slow and hard until he filled her insides tightly. "Ooooh yesss…that's what it do, Papiiiii…fuck me…yes." She moaned and cried out in pleasure until she exploded and collapsed on Chio's chest. He hugged her and continued to pump inside of her causing her to convulse with a second orgasm. The Hurricane kept his penis hard and he wouldn't cum until his high wore off, much like the effects of ecstasy. Kitty loved when he made love to her when he was high because when he was sober his sex game was weak to her. He always came too quick when he wasn't high.

"Mami, we're going to New York, next week for a party my dude Diablo Black is giving so go buy yourself something pretty to wear. I want to show you off. I'll also have your publicist set up some interviews for you B.E.T. and M.T.V. and some press. I'm gonna blow your shit up in NY then we'll set up a tour for you."

"Papi, thank you." Kitty squealed giddy with excitement.

"Whoo wee calm down girl. I can think of a better way to thank me than all that noise you're making." Chio grinned devilishly, pushing Kitty's head down his body. She didn't need any guidance—she gladly showed him how grateful she was for everything..

CHAPTER 22

The Hamptons, a very affluent exclusive neighborhood on Long Island, New York was home to the super wealthy. At one time, it was exclusive to the Uber rich white society until the influx of wealthy African American entertainers and industry moguls invaded the island. Needless to say, the old money, blue bloods were mortified.

Diablo and Gazelle owned a magnificent estate off the beach in Sag Harbor. True to her word Gazelle took Mafia and Daisy via her private helicopter to her summer home in the Hamptons for their retreat. Diablo stayed at their townhouse in the city so she had the mansion to herself and planned to show the girls a good time. Gazelle was attracted to Daisy and couldn't wait to get her away from her cousin. She had very little patience and wanted what she wanted now. Daisy drove Gazelle wild with lust. Her stunning beauty and vibrant personality made Gazelle's mouth water. It took everything out of her not to stare at Daisy during the ride. She caught herself when Mafia glared at her for not paying attention to what she was saying. Gazelle quickly played it off like she was in deep thought—she couldn't let Mafia get a whiff of her attraction to her cousin. That would be a disaster. She wouldn't be able to handle it, not only was Mafia insanely jealous but she had no idea Gazelle slept around on her—not to mention cheating on her with her cousin would be a violation.

Gazelle was moist between her thighs just thinking about the danger involved with creeping off in her forty room mansion to make love to the lovely southern belle. She had no idea if Daisy was even remotely interested in a female sexual liaison. That small fact was irrelevant to Gazelle because she had never been rejected, besides her gaydar buzzed softly when she was around Daisy. She had a particular look in her alluring green eyes that was very familiar to Gazelle. Daisy Jones was a freak and Gazelle was determined to bring that freak front and center before the weekend was over.

Daisy unpacked her Christian Dior carrier and settled in the guest suite Gazelle assigned her. She was impressed with the singer's home. *Gazelle's mansion could sure give Chio a run for his money*, Daisy thought. Daisy's room was heavenly. The high vaulted ceiling was airbrushed with floating clouds on a peaceful pale blue sky. Her bed was a white marble canopy with a beautiful white down comforter and had a dozen fluffy down filled pillows. The walls were painted with images of baby angels sailing across the skies playing harps. She had never seen such majestic decor in a bedroom before. Her feet sunk two inches into the soft, plush white carpet. Daisy truly felt like she was in heaven. She walked out to the balcony overlooking the beach and stood in awe of the view. *Damn, Gazelle is a lucky woman,* thought Daisy enviously. She would have loved to trade places with the superstar and be the queen of her castle.

Gazelle had no idea Daisy was being groomed by Diablo to replace her. Daisy grinned—it would be no time before she would be living lavishly and if it meant knocking Gazelle off her throne then so be it. Daisy didn't feel guilty in the slightest. She had to look out for herself and get what she deserved, by all means, necessary, and besides she was helping out her cousin and family always came first. Mama Jones always told her to be a queen she had to live like one and she had finally found her king. Diablo Black was going to be hers and she didn't care that he had a little sugar in his tank because she had no intention of letting him touch her. She wasn't crazy. It was no telling what he had contracted sleeping with men or whatever he did with them. *Yuck,* she thought. The weird thing was the funny looks Gazelle had been giving her. If she didn't know better she would have thought she wanted to fuck her. She shook her long wild curls and twirled around giggling at the thought. She wouldn't mind giving Ms. Superstar a taste of her goldmine but she didn't want to hurt her cousin. She knew Mafia was deeply in love with Gazelle and she didn't want to go there. But if the sexy star kept giving her goo-goo eyes, it was going to be hard to resist. Daisy felt the sexual tension and she was horny as hell.

She missed Chio's bomb ass head and how he used to suck fire out of her. Daisy crawled into the inviting bed and began stroking herself imagining Chio's tongue gliding over her clit. She was in her bra and panties and slid her panties off and cocked her legs open just as she was ready to explode Gazelle popped her head into the room without knocking. She was surprised and immediately aroused at the sight of Daisy masturbating. Her Brazilian waxed cunt was very enticing. Gazelle silently crawled over to the large bed and crept up the side of the mattress. Daisy's eyes were closed as she caressed herself lovingly deep in the throes of passion. Gazelle was mesmerized and couldn't stop herself she gently eased on the bed and slid her face between Daisy's legs. She kissed her fingers and nudged them aside with her tongue. Daisy jumped, startled by the intrusion, but she overcame the shock when she saw Gazelle's head buried in her cunt. She grabbed her head forcefully and humped her face until she came, Daisy was wild with lust and dazed by Gazelle's brazen boldness. She was completely stunned and couldn't believe what had happened.

Daisy Jones was getting head from the megastar Gazelle who was adored and worshipped by millions. Just the thought alone made Daisy bust, shivering sensually while another orgasm coursed through her body. Gazelle lapped her juices up like a St. Bernard. Without uttering a word she eased up, rolled off the bed and sashayed out the door. Daisy was dumbfounded.

The rest of the weekend Daisy avoided Gazelle, pretending to have a stomach virus. She managed to stay in the bed until they were ready to leave. She was too ashamed to face Mafia and she didn't want to be alone with Gazelle. She fantasized about her the whole weekend. She wanted more. Gazelle made her feel amazing and she was very addictive, but Daisy knew she was playing with fire and decided she didn't want to get burnt, so she fought the craving for more and stayed out of the way. She knew her passion wasn't worth Mafia's wrath or pain. Daisy didn't know what Mafia would do if she ever found out what jumped off between her and Gazelle and she didn't want to find out. Mafia wasn't the least bit suspicious. She felt bad for Daisy's sudden illness but was secretly happy she could enjoy Gazelle's company all by herself. They had a ball together Gazelle was in wonderful spirits. She was happy that she was able to creep with Daisy and didn't dare try for more as bad as she wanted to. Mafia was all over her and she was satisfied. Daisy was a treat, but Mafia was her main course and by the end of the weekend she was full.

By the time they arrived back into the city, the girls were relaxed and well rested. Daisy couldn't wait to get back into the studio with Diablo. He had no idea she had spent the weekend at his mansion in the Hamptons and she didn't plan to tell him. She knew for certain his wife wouldn't mention it so she was caught completely off guard when he invited her to join him for a few days back to the Hamptons. She was speechless but managed not to give it away that she had already been to his house. Gazelle was leaving to begin her promotional tour and Diablo said he wanted to finish recording Daisy at his Hamptons in-house studio. Daisy repacked and told Mafia where she was off to. "Girl you won't believe this, Diablo is flying back to the Hamptons to finish recording me," gushed Daisy. Things were moving so fast her head was spinning.

"That's what's up. He is feeling you. I knew you could get that nigga nose open. He must be tired of Gazelle. I hope so," Mafia said gleefully.

"He said I am a natural born star," bragged Daisy.

"You are…that you are. Now I need you to get an Oscar because I want him so Daisytised that he forgets who the hell Gazelle is," joked Mafia.

"I'm on it, Cuz, don't worry about a thing," Daisy assured her cousin she had no doubts about the takeover. She wanted it all—the success, fame and all the fortune because ultimately she wanted to destroy Young Chio and his whore. She needed money and power to take them down and she wouldn't stop until she succeeded and Diablo was the key to her success.

CHAPTER 23

Anjel missed Daisy but was happy for her good fortune. Daisy called her to fill her in on Diablo and her new singing career. Anjel laughed at the idea of Daisy singing. She had never heard her sing seriously, but leave it to Daisy to go to New York and walk right into a record deal without even trying. Classic, Daisy Jones. Anjel wished she had luck like that, but as long as her body stayed tight and kept her sex game right she would be a star in her world. Fucking was her talent and she was triple platinum on all the charts. Anjel giggled and prepared herself for work. When she walked on stage she was delighted to see the Black Columbian Cartel walk through the door of the club. As soon as she spotted Geechi she went into super freak mode and signaled to the DJ to throw on her favorite song, *Angel* by Anita Baker.

She wore a silver g-string with Diamond rhinestones that decorated her crotch area. She had matching diamond pasties stuck on her nipples. Her body shimmered with diamond dust glitter every time she slid up and down the pole. The strobe lights in the club reflected off her body giving her the illusion of a glowing snake, the way she writhed and slithered across the stage until she was directly in front of Geechi. Their eyes locked and sparks flew. Geechi stood over Anjel's shimmery body and rained a bucket of hundred dollar bills all over her glowing frame. Anjel instantly became moist, she did a slow sensual body flip rolling her hips and spreading her legs so he could see the juices from her hot box flowing for him. He fingered her gently and brought his cum covered fingers to his nose and took a deep whiff. He smiled slowly appreciating the fresh scent.

"Let's go to the champagne room," he mouthed. Anjel couldn't wait—she picked up her cash and obediently followed Geechi. She would have paid him to fuck her—that's how bad she wanted him. She only wished she could have videotaped their freak session when it was over. She wanted to show it to Ivy. That would teach that bitch not to roll up on her over no nigga ever again. Anjel's revenge was sweeter than any poison Ivy could ever dish out.

She smiled smugly as she rode Geechi's dick like a thoroughbred. *This nigga is a keeper*, she thought, delirious from the waves of pleasure he gave her with each stroke.

CHAPTER 24

CoCo was happy to be back in New York. She and Ivy were having a prosperous day and were in high spirits. They stole about twenty thousand dollars worth of merchandise from Short Hills Mall in New Jersey. The girls loved the affluent suburban mall it reminded them of the Lenox Mall in Atlanta, minus the black shoppers. Short Hills shoppers were predominantly white and very rich. Ivy and CoCo dressed up and fit in nicely. They looked like the basketball wives that shopped there who were married to the New Jersey Nets. They both carried expensive Louis Vuitton bags with matching wallets. Ivy believed in presentation and made a show of setting her four thousand dollar purse on the counter and pulled out her thousand dollar wallet slowly selecting one of the illegal credit cards she used to purchase her items. The cashiers rarely if ever asked for identification and when they did she had one ready that matched every identity that she assumed. She was on top of her game and loved to con people into giving her whatever she wanted. Everything went smoothly that day until they hit the last spot, Neiman Marcus.

Ivy sent CoCo to the rental to put the shopping bags away. She never carried more than one shopping bag into a store, especially in a mall. She didn't want to arouse suspicion by carrying a million bags from store to store. The mall security cameras were trained to spot suspicious behavior and that was a tip-off. CoCo was ready to leave. She felt bad vibes, but Ivy insisted in going in Neiman Marcus she was so caught up in the moment that she actually started to believe that she was shopping with her own money—a mistake she would learn to regret.

CoCo returned from the parking lot and met Ivy on the main level of the department store. Ivy was in the Prada section by the door nearest where their rental was parked. The store was quiet and half empty sprinkled with only a few shoppers. Ivy handed her credit card to the middle-aged snooty white saleswoman who suddenly started walking to the back area reserved for employees. "Um excuse me, Ma'am, where are you going with my card?" Ivy asked coolly.

"I'll be right back Mrs. Goldwyn," replied the sales lady referring to the name that was on Ivy's card and continued to walk briskly to the private office. CoCo peeped the situation and felt even stronger vibes to get the hell out of there.

"Ivy let's get the fuck outta here—the spot is blown up," whispered CoCo nervously.

"Chill I got this. Go get the car and meet me by the exit," ordered Ivy coolly.

"OK, but your ass is crazy. That old lady is on some sneaky shit." Coco didn't bother to wait for a response she headed to the exit praying she made it out the store without security running up on her. Ivy looked around to make sure there was no security in the area and followed the old lady through the door, disregarding the fact that she wasn't supposed to be behind there. She was on the woman's heels and caught her with the phone in her hand calling security.

"Uh-uh, bitch," snarled Ivy as she snatched the phone out of the woman's hand.

"I beg your pardon Ms. you are not allowed back here and I am calling security," the woman shrieked in panic. Ivy snatched the phone from the ladies gnarled wrinkled hand and grabbed her in a headlock. She had the poor woman in a death grip and didn't release her until she felt her slump weakly against her and slide to the floor. She made her pass out by blocking her air supply. Geechi had done it to her plenty of times. She wasn't worried about the old bag. She figured she would wake up in a few minutes and by that time Ivy and CoCo would be long gone. Ivy calmly walked back out to the front and picked up her Prada bag she was trying to purchase and put it in a shopping bag. She threw two more of the costly bags in her shopping bag and walked smoothly to the exit. If she was being watched it would be near impossible for the observer to know that she had damn near killed the sales lady and boldly continued to steal as she left the crime scene. Ivy had a set of balls on her that were made of cast iron. She had no conscience and was scared of nothing or no one. She was carefree as she sauntered out of the store and jumped into the waiting car. CoCo was on point and pulled off instantly. Before Ivy could tell her what happened in the mall a security truck was behind them flashing sirens, signaling them to pull over. CoCo looked at Ivy expectedly and Ivy gave her a look that meant business.

"Drive. Don't stop for anyone. Push this shit. Let's goooo," she shouted, snapping CoCo out of the terror that had her stuck. She knew Anthony and her family would kill her if she got arrested again. They had over fifty credit cards with matching fake IDs in their possession. Not to mention all the stolen goods that loaded their rental's trunk. She had no choice but to keep driving. She couldn't afford to get caught. She had no idea that they were running from something far more serious. The attempted murder charge they faced would have brought her panic to hysteria. CoCo dipped and swerved through the maze of cars in the narrow parking lot and shot out of the mall with the security truck racing behind them. The girls heard sirens quickly approaching and knew shit was about to hit the fan. The toy cops weren't the problem anymore—the Police were on their trail. "Turn left," Ivy screamed. "Now right...No, no. Don't go on the highway. Stay on the back roads. They will think we jumped on the highway."

CoCo deftly made a few sharp turns and managed to shake the cops. They heard the screeching wails of the sirens fading in the quietness of the suburban neighborhood. Ivy's adrenaline was pumping. She was scared and excited. CoCo was terrified and practically quivering in her seat but she drove the rental like she was in an Indy 500

"We lost them. You a bad bitch. You drove the shit out of this whip. Park right here just in case they bring the choppers out to look for us," instructed Ivy. CoCo pulled over and parked on a quiet street with four other minivans. The rented minivan fit right in with the other vehicles and they blended right in. She cut the engine and they climbed in the back and hid under the seats for five hours before they felt safe. By the time they made it back to the hotel they were sweaty and dirty and a ball of frazzled nerves. "Girl, I 'shoulda stayed my black ass in Atlanta," CoCo complained. "I can't afford to catch a case. I came up here to party, not go to jail," she said sucking her teeth. She was pissed off because if Ivy wouldn't have been so greedy all the drama could have been avoided. She still didn't know what Ivy did to the saleslady. Ivy didn't even bother to tell her. She knew CoCo would freak out and she didn't feel like hearing all the bitchin about nothing.

"Oh, bitch, pleezzz you wasn't saying all that when you were buying shit with my work. You know the risk you were taking when you were hustling, so cut the shit hoe," Ivy smirked meanly. It was business as usual—for Ivy going to jail was the occupational hazard of a hustler. She would do whatever was necessary to keep her freedom including hurting anyone that tried to send her to jail, old people could get it too, she chuckled thinking about how she duffed out the old biddy at the store.

Poison Ivy was a lunatic and wouldn't hesitate to kill anyone that got in her way. It was a little after 11 p.m. when the girls had showered and settled down in their luxury suite. They were waiting for room service to bring their food, they were starving and seriously in the need of a bottle of wine with a good steak to calm their nerves. Ivy rolled up a blunt while CoCo sorted their stolen goods. The living room was filled with designer clothes, shoes and accessories scattered all over the place. CoCo was sufficiently checked by Ivy and finally relaxed and enjoyed trying on all her new fly gear. "Damn, Ivy we came off. I have been trying to get this Chanel dress for the longest. I think I'm going to wear this to Diablo's party what do you think?"

"Naw it's too boring. You need something like my *Alexander Mcqueen* dress. I'm gonna kill them when I rock this," bragged Ivy. She was feeling untouchable and didn't care what anyone thought. In her mind, she was the baddest chick on the planet. She lived life like a celebrity. Her lifestyle was just as lavish as any famous person and she was a legend in the streets. She was a certified OBG and loved it.

"Pass me my red bottoms these babies are hot," said Ivy lovingly, stroking the fifteen hundred dollar Christian Louboutin shoes.

"Those are killers but my Prada pumps are sicker," said CoCo.

"Bitch you bugging my..." Ivy was interrupted by a knock on the door. "Oh good. It's the food. A bitch is starving." she trotted over to the door and flung it open.

"Freeze, bitch. Get on the floor. Now." a burly black cop ordered, barging into the room followed by a team of police. Ivy was stunned and too shocked to move. The cop slammed her roughly against the wall while two other cops bum-rushed CoCo and had her handcuffed in a matter of seconds. CoCo was speechless she knew their asses were done. She found out just how done they were when they arrived at the police station.

Apparently, the credit card Ivy used to charge the suite was blown up. She spent so much money off of the card that she caused a red flag to go up. Fifty thousand in four days was an unusual spending habit for the real Margaret Von Baron so the credit card company contacted her and began tracking down the impersonator starting with the hotel she charged using Margaret's card. The police investigated the trail of credit cards they found in the girl's possession and linked them to the attempted murder of the Neiman Marcus sales lady in Short Hills Mall. If that wasn't enough, when they fingerprinted Ivy a warrant for murder popped up for the drug dealer she killed in Brooklyn. The detectives on the case found evidence to charge her with the body. She was charged with murder in the first degree, attempted murder, 120 counts of credit card fraud, identity theft, kidnapping, and assault in the second degree. Ivy was devastated when they charged her with the beating and kidnapping of Tela—the girl they tortured so many years ago.

The detectives wanted CoCo to testify against Ivy. She contemplated it for a millisecond because she was so furious with her for not telling her about the old lady she almost killed. They were charging her as an accomplice to the attempted murder charge. She didn't know how she was going to explain that to her family. She had done some crazy shit before but this took the cake. She wanted to cry and she wanted her twin so bad. She sat stonily in the cold interrogation room in silence. She thought long and hard while the detectives droned on and on about how much time she was going to get and she decided that although Ivy was a greedy, grimy, crazy bitch she would remain loyal to her—after all she was an OBG and she would die before she disgraced herself or her clique by becoming a cheese eating rat. She had "death before dishonor" tattooed on her arm. She stared at her tat long and hard before she gave the detectives her answer. She cleared her throat and the detectives fell silent "I want three things," she whispered.

"Give us what we want and you got it, Kid," one of the detectives piped, eager to cut a deal with CoCo. They wanted to know who supplied the girls with the credit cards and they were willing to cut CoCo loose if she gave up that information and testify against Ivy. "I want a phone call. I want my lawyer and I want you to go fuck yourself," smirked CoCo defiantly. The detective's faces fell and they walked out of the tiny dimly lit room without saying a word. They were determined to bury both of the girls.

CHAPTER 25

Anthony Davis flew to New York as soon as he heard about CoCo's arrest. He couldn't believe the serious charges she was being held on. He knew one day his bad ass cousins would get into something that they couldn't get out of. Casey was devastated and insisted on coming with him to help her twin sister. They arrived in the city the weekend of Diablo Black's birthday party. When they checked into the Marriott Hotel they bumped into Young Chio and Kitty in the lobby "What up with you my dude? You up here for Black's Party?" Chio asked Anthony excitedly.

"Naw homie, I forgot all about that. Tell you the truth my people got into some shit, so I'm up here taking care of that, but I can't make any moves until Monday. So I might swing thru —where is it going to be?"

"It's at a penthouse on 72nd Street and Park Avenue. It's a black tie affair—you know that nigga on some Hollywood shit.

I hear Jay-Z might perform for that nigga. You know his shit is going to be off da hook. I want to see if his shit is crunk, like how we do the damn thing in the A," said Chio cockily. He respected Diablo and was secretly in awe of all the star power his event attracted, but he would never admit it.

"I don't know about that but I'm gonna stop by and check it out how 'bout it, Casey?" "

"Yeah, I guess it doesn't make any sense to mope around all weekend," said Casey sadly. CoCo and Ivy were being held without bail, so their only hope was the best defense possible. Anthony paid for CoCo's lawyer and Geechi was supposed to pay for Ivy's, but so far Casey hadn't heard from him. Ivy was stressing because he was ducking her calls. Casey felt sorry for her because she heard rumors that he was fucking with Anjel hard and was shitting on Ivy.

"My new artist will be performing at the party too," Chio said proudly, pointing at Kitty. She looked fabulous, like a bona fide diva. She smiled coolly and greeted Anthony and CoCo briefly before turning her attention back to her cell phone. Kitty was star tripping and feeling herself big time. Chio had created a monster. He didn't notice her new attitude. He was too busy lusting over her sexy luscious body clad in a white catsuit. Anthony was too stressed over his lil' cousin's predicament to care about Kitty's stank attitude, but Casey glared at her with disgust. This was the same hoe that Daisy bloodied in the club acting like she was all that. Casey thought ready to jump in dat ass but she controlled herself. It wasn't the time or the place.

She would definitely catch her later on at the party. She mentally promised Kitty an ass whooping. Casey was missing her twin and had zero tolerance for any bullshit. They both cried for fifteen minutes when CoCo called her from Riker's Island. They were lost and miserable without each other and anyone was liable to get it the way Casey felt.

"Alright, I'll catch up with you later. We gotta get something to wear," said Anthony, glancing at Casey hoping the mention of shopping would brighten her spirits. Casey was so zoned out she didn't even hear him. Anthony gave Chio a parting dap and guided Casey to their suite. Young Chio and Kitty were off to promote Kitty's album. MTV was going to be in the building so Kitty's showcase performance had to be dead right so she could get positive press. Everything was going as Chio planned it. Kitty was heading straight for stardom.

Daisy was a bundle of nerves Diablo wanted her to perform at his party that night and she was sick with fear. When he told her that Chio's artist Kitty was performing, too she could have died. She was mortified of bombing in front of her arch enemies. She was going to lip sync so there would be no mistakes. She had practiced her routine with her band and dancers until she had it down pat. Not only was Kitty performing but some other guest celebrities were going to drop by too and were scheduled to perform. Diablo assured her she would be fine. He had no idea about her relationship with Young Chio and what she did to Kitty.

Diablo adored Daisy; they grew close very quickly. She had a ball in the Hamptons with him. She cooked him delicious southern meals that Diablo devoured. They got along great and Daisy was disappointed about his down low lifestyle and was starting to doubt it was true. He certainly didn't act like a homo thug. He tried to have sex with her, but of course, she shut him down with the virginity excuse. He was shocked as usual, but he respected her and it kept him at bay. It didn't deter him from treating her like a queen and turning her into a decent singer. He brought in a voice coach for her and before she knew it she was hitting notes she never dreamed she could sing. She loved Diablo for what he was doing for her and they became very good friends. Daisy decided to ask him about his rumored sexuality—she couldn't help herself, she just had to know—he was too damn fine and a true gentleman. "Big Daddy can I ask you a question?" she said timidly.

"Ask me anything baby girl," replied Diablo lovingly.

"Uh, are you…I mean—do you go both ways?" asked Daisy, regretting immediately asking the blasphemous question. It felt like time stopped and everything went still. Daisy literally felt the chilly icy cold tension in the air. Diablo glared at her with fire in his eyes

"Don't ever disrespect me like that again. I won't even insult myself by answering that bullshit," he barked roughly. Daisy saw a different side of Diablo and it shook her. She didn't say a word. She got up and left the room, quickly getting dressed for the party. She fiddled nervously with her hair when Diablo came up behind her quietly. "Baby girl, never believe the garbage you hear in this industry about me or anybody else. This is a cutthroat business and the best way to assassinate someone's character is to question their manhood. I never was or will be a crap shooter. OK?" Diablo rubbed Daisy's shoulders waiting for her response to the self-righteous game he spit at her. He was a cool cucumber acting his butt off because he knew damn well he played with the boys once in a while.

"I'm sorry, Diablo. I didn't really believe it—I just had to ask you for myself," quivered Daisy on the verge of tears. She didn't want to turn him off after all he had done for her.

"I know, baby. I overreacted. I'm glad you brought this to my attention and we cleared the air. Now finish getting ready—we have a big night ahead of us." Diablo left Daisy to finish getting ready. He bought her a beautiful Rachel Roy dress that fit her like a glove. It was a shimmering gold lame mini and looked absolutely stunning on her. She rubbed gold flecks of glitter from body lotion on her arms and shapely legs. She set off her look with matching gold studded stilettos. She pinned her long curls up and let a few tendrils fall, framing her pretty face. When Diablo saw her he was mesmerized by her beauty and knew he had found the perfect replacement for his wife and he didn't hold her stupid question against her—after all, he was lying through his teeth. He loved men but would deny it until the day he died.

CHAPTER 26

Geechi and Anjel were going strong. He was feeling her so much that he made her stop stripping. He only allowed her to perform for him and his boys. She didn't have a problem with it because she made more money dancing privately than she ever made for the club. When she heard about Ivy getting trapped off in New York she was determined to become his new Wifey. Anjel knew he loved her because he never let any of his friends disrespect her. She belonged to him and she loved it. Anjel asked Geechi to come with her to New York to see Daisy perform at Diablo's birthday party and he agreed. He knew about the big event and he and his crew were planning on going to the bash anyway. He rented a private jet to fly him and his boys up north. Anjel flew into the city in style. She was so excited and always wanted to be a member of the mile high club that she wasted no time fucking Geechi's brains out as they soared through the clouds.

Geechi's phone vibrated as Anjel was riding him, interrupting their session. He glanced at his cell and shook his head in annoyance. "I wish this bitch stop calling my jack. I ain't got nuttin' for her ass. She in too deep I can't go nowhere near her, she's hot, dem boys done picked up her shit," he ranted, referring to the feds involved in Ivy's cases.

"Fuck her, she probably tryna tell them boys all she knows about you to get outta that shit," Anjel instigated.

"That's why I'm staying outta that shit. She up on a murder beef, that shit is serious, they fittin' to lay her ass down she on her own," Geechi stated coldly. He didn't want anything to do with Ivy since her arrest, after the first call when she was crying hysterically and begged him to get her a lawyer. He told her he would, but after he heard how serious her charges were he decided the thirty thousand the lawyer wanted for her case was a waste of money. The feds had picked up her case and the government had a 99 percent conviction rate. Her ass was grass simple as that.

Geechi didn't give Ivy another thought. He simply replaced her with Anjel. She wasn't as thorough as Ivy but at least she wasn't hustling and getting into trouble. He didn't have to worry about constantly bailing her out of jail. He was tired of street girls and was ready to find a housewife. If Anjel wasn't a hoe she would have been perfect. Geechi glanced at Anjel and shook his head. He refused to let his dick make decisions for him. He wasn't about to turn a hoe into a housewife. Anjel would be his ride or die bitch; nothing more, nothing less.

The BCC was ready to get their party on the guys were popping bottles and enjoying the flight on the luxury jet. Anjel was the Cartel's mascot, so to speak. She provided the entertainment and loved being the only female aboard the jet because of all the attention she received. She worked them into a sexual frenzy with an erotic striptease. Geechi pulled her back down on his lap and she' rode him like a stallion until he exploded inside of her while the crew cheered him on wildly. They became rowdy pulling and rubbing on Anjel's naked body. She suddenly got scared and looked at Geechi. One look at his gorgeous face and she was ready to do anything to please him. Even if it meant servicing his entire crew. He hypnotized her with his chinky eyes, gazing at her like she was the sexiest woman on the planet. She relaxed and gave in to the squeezes and probes from the horny guys.

Geechi roared suddenly "Get the fuck off off her. She's off limits." The touching and rowdy cat calls ceased immediately. Geechi picked Anjel up and carried her to the small bedroom cabin in the rear of the plane. He laid her down and made passionate love to her. "You're mine," he whispered, plunging deeply inside of her. Anjel felt his passion and had never felt so wanted in her life. She was ready to die for Geechi and had finally found the love she had been searching for since her mother died. It wasn't perfect or traditional, but she felt like she was on top of the world and she was just fine with what it was. She was happy.

CHAPTER 27

Mafia was so upset over Ivy's arrest that she almost didn't go to Diablo's party, but she promised Daisy and didn't want to let her down. Mafia couldn't believe Ivy was being charged for shit they did back in the days. She also knew that meant the feds wanted her, too, for her involvement in kidnapping and assaulting Tela. Mafia made arrangements for the best attorney in New York to represent Ivy since the bitch ass nigga she was going out with left her for dead. Mafia had her partner's back. Death before Dishonor, all day every day. Ivy didn't need to depend on anybody as long as she had her OBG's. They stuck by each other no matter what.

Mafia was going to turn herself in and have her attorney get her a bail. She didn't need the feds looking for her and discover she was running a million dollar drug operation. She'd rather face the kidnapping and assault charges than open up a can of even bigger worms. Her head was spinning, her Homie was facing life in prison and she would have to fight a case that could put her away for a decade. She was flabbergasted at how quickly her life was shook upside down. It seemed like her whole team would be locked up soon. Mistress was already doing a five-year bid and now Ivy. Mafia felt sick. She stopped getting dressed so she could smoke a blunt to calm her nerves. She wanted Gazelle, but she was on tour overseas.

Mafia decided to call NellyPop and Asia so they could be on point. After warning the other girls and bringing them up to speed with Ivy's situation she finished getting dressed. The marijuana mellowed her out and she drank Patron straight from the bottle. *I might as well party hard before I turn myself in*, she thought. Then another thought entered her head, *Fuck outta here. I'm not turning myself in before I find Tela and get rid of her. No victim. No conviction.* Mafia grinned devilishly and threw on her platinum iced out OBG chain. She looked in the mirror and admired her sexy image, she wore her hair straight with a part in the middle and she even put on some mascara and eyeliner to make her eyes pop out. She did the makeup on special occasions and had to admit she looked very exotic when she was in fem mode. She wore a fitted *VelvetStar* denim jumper and knee-high leather Stilettos she was killing 'em. She took another long swig of Patron and a deep drag off her blunt and headed out the door. She couldn't wait to see Daisy perform. She felt much better and was ready to get her party on. She invited NellyPop and Asia and couldn't wait to see her girls. She needed to vibe with her clique so they could come up with a plan to track Tela down and eliminate their problem.

CHAPTER 28

Labasia, Tajil, and Miosha were excited and proud of their girl, Daisy. She had invited them to the party and they were more than happy to fly up to New York and cheer her on and party with the A-list crowd. "Miss Thang this gala is ovah. Mr. Black bettaaa worrrkkk," said Labasia in her drama queen voice. She loved the lavishly decorated townhouse. The theme of the party was reminiscent of the Roman Empire period. There were women with gold sprayed leaves covering their breasts and private areas, serving champagne and caviar.

"Chile, look at all these fine men up in here. I need to find a hot boy tonight because my panties are dripping," Labasia squealed outrageously. Miosha and Tajil burst out laughing.

"Girl shut up, I need one too," said Miosha. She was so gorgeous you would think it wouldn't be hard for her to find a good man, but it seemed like she intimidated most men. She was so tired of ninety-day relationships and she wanted to start a family. Miosha and her motley crew scanned the crowd closely, looking for Daisy, anxious to see their friend.

Mafia arrived with a few of the OBG's ready to have a ball. It felt so good to hang out with her childhood friends. It had been a while since they partied together. They still lived in the projects and was as ghetto as ever. She loved them because it was refreshing to be around some real chicks. She was so sick of all the fake bougie people in the industry. A lot of them forgot where they came from. Nelly and Asia loved Brooklyn and never left their beloved borough.

NellyPop was a booster and although she was fly she still had trouble finding an outfit to fit around her 44F breasts and wore ill fitted clothes. She had on a dress that was at least two sizes too small. Her gigantic breast was spilling out of the tiny dress. She was very petite, she stood 4'10" and very rough around the edges. Her braided extensions were neat, but she had no edges around her hairline. Her eyes were pretty and slightly slanted, but her skin was riddled with acne. She stayed in name brand outfits to disguise her flaws, sometimes it worked sometimes it didn't. That night it didn't she looked a hot mess.

Asia, on the other hand, looked much better, she was also petite but unlike her friend she was easier on the eyes, flawless beige skin and pretty white teeth made her face stand out. She wore a spandex catsuit that fit her full figure nicely. She had a little pouch belly, but her ass was so thick that it was all you noticed on her short frame. Her only downfall was she cursed like a sailor. She was the queen of cursing somebody the fuck out. She coined the term I'mma cuss, somebody, the fuck out,' that's all she ever said. The girls never changed and although they were all in their early thirties they still were as wild as they were in their teens.

NellyPop had snuck her .22 two-shooter into the party. She had it stuffed in her panties. She stayed strapped and carried her gun everywhere she went. Asia had her blade in her mouth ready to spit it out at a moment's notice. Mafia got a kick out of her OBG's from the hood. It was nothing like the original crew and would never get too big to hang with her original clique. She had recruited a whole new team since she moved to Harlem. Her new girls had a little more finesse than her Brooklyn faction. They were more laid back whereas the Brooklyn OBG's were buck wild. The new Crew was ballers, not brawlers. If she needed to put in work she called on her go get 'em girls' from Brooklyn.

Her right-hand girl, Kadijah had 125th Street on lock. She distributed all types of tropical exotic marijuana by the pound. Mafia met her when she copped some pounds from her and the two became fast friends. After doing business for a few months Mafia put Kadijah down with the OBG's. Then there was her driver/security Sassy. Mafia never went anywhere without Sassy short for Assassin. She was an ex-marine home on a medical discharge for losing half her earlobe by a sniper's bullet in Iraq. They met through a mutual friend. Sassy needed a job and Mafia needed a driver. When she met Sassy and reviewed her credentials it was a done deal. Sassy carried a Nine Millimeter

Glock and was a black belt in martial arts, which Mafia loved because she couldn't carry her gun legally, because of her prior felony. She kept Sassy close by in case she had to have her bust her gun legally for her.

Kadijah and Sassy were as different as night and day. Kadijah was 6'0" with a boyish build. She was cute but had a very serious demeanor. Sassy was a white girl with a slim physique and an innocent face that belied her killer instincts. She was soft-spoken, a true example of bad girls who moved in silence. She loved Mafia and was loyal to the death because Mafia was the only one to give her a job when she came back from Iraq. Even the government abandoned her and she regretted putting her life on the line for her country. The country didn't seem to give a damn about her and no one appreciated the sacrifices she made in the war. If it wasn't for Mafia she would have to rely on her disability check. As soon as she got down with Mafia she got her own whip, jewelry, nice clothes and access to star-studded dick. Sassy loved working for Mafia and would kill for her if anyone tried to violate her boss.

Mafia and her crew headed to the bar and ordered a couple of bottles of Ciroc and Nuvo. Mafia was so proud of Daisy and wanted to celebrate her cousin's new career. She knew Daisy was a bad bitch but not only did she succeed in getting Diablo open she managed to get a record deal from him as well. All Mafia could say was, "Wow." She knew Gazelle was going to have a fit when she found out Daisy was signed to Diablo's label. The thought of her reaction put a smile on Mafia's face.

She knew her well enough to know that she wasn't going to play seconds to Daisy. She would leave Diablo first and that's just what Mafia wanted her to do. It was a win, win situation. Daisy got a career and Mafia would have her woman. Mafia was thrilled.

"Let's toast to my cousin, Daisy Jones. She is definitely a bad bitch. She came up here for a visit and got herself a deal. Now tell me that ain't a bad bitch," Mafia said, clinking her champagne glass against the other girl's. The girls drank and gave up props to Daisy as Anjel and Casey approached the jubilant group. "Oh shit, you must be Daisy's cousin, Mafia. Hey, girl, I'm Anjel, Daisy's best friend and this is Casey"

"My sister is locked up with Poison Ivy. We are both OBG's from the Atlanta faction," Casey stated proudly. Mafia jumped up and gave both girls a hug

"What's up, Shorty. Ivy told me all about y'all. That's fucked up what happened to them. I am sick over that shit. I'm sorry to hear about your twin. Ivy said she's a trooper, tho' you already know how we represent OBG for life," Mafia said, prompting the girls to toast the fallen OBG's. "Where is Daisy?" Mafia asked Anjel.

"She is getting ready for the show. She doesn't want to make an appearance until show time."

"That's my girl. She is a superstar already," Mafia said, bragging. Before the girls could make another toast the half-naked hostesses began ushering the party goers to the main hall where the performances were being held. Diablo had really outdone himself with the party. He had an elaborate ice sculpture designed like a naked goddess with champagne flowing from the nipples of the masterpiece. The ritzy townhouse was transformed into a Roman palace. He had a different DJ in every room. DJ Khaled was spinning for the showcase and had the crowd jamming to his single, *Welcome to my Hood,* as the room filled to capacity he wished Diablo a happy birthday and brought him out on the stage. "Give it up for my man the infamous Diablo Black." The crowd went wild. Diablo sauntered out enjoying the love he received from his friends and associates. His powerful frame was draped in a three-piece grey suit his shoes were a darker shade of grey crocodile skin that came alive as he stepped into the stage light. He was sharp as a tack and knew it, he had on a matching grey crocodile Derby tilted on his head and diamond encrusted cufflinks to match the dazzling stones blinging in his pinky ring.

Diablo grinned as he waited for the thunderous applause to die down. "I want to thank all of you for the love and well wishes and for sharing my special day with me. I am very pleased to announce I have a new edition to my label. Her name is Daisy Jones and I want y'all to show her some love," Diablo said as he stepped off the stage and Daisy appeared. The spotlight shined on her and her pretty dancers and she ran through her choreographed routine. Daisy danced and lip-synced her heart out. Her recorded vocals were clear and she moved so well that it was virtually unnoticeable that she wasn't actually singing. She had pulled it off and she beamed with pride as she strutted her stuff on stage. She was on top of the world and she wanted to scream, *Look at me now, nicca*, right in Chio's face before she hog spit.

CHAPTER 29

Kitty and Chio stood in disbelief as they gawked with their mouth's open at Daisy while she performed on stage. "Hell no that bitch can't sing," Kitty seethed and stormed over to the DJ booth. Chio followed behind her. She eased into the booth with the DJ and asked him a question she already knew the answer for. When he confirmed she grinned evilly. She told Chio

"She's lip syncing."

"Oh yeah? I got a trick for that bitch." He dug into his pocket and pulled off fifty-one hundred dollar bills and handed them to the DJ. "Make her CD skip. Consider this a personal favor." Chio eyed the DJ confidently, knowing that his greed would give in to his request. The DJ looked at the money, stuffed it in his pocket and nodded his head. Before Chio or Kitty could say another word Daisy was standing on the stage holding her mike with a panic-stricken look on her face. Her music was skipping and her vocals kept repeating the same lyrics. Her dancers quickly exited the stage, leaving her standing alone looking quite stupid facing the crowd. It was every singer's worst nightmare, especially if they really couldn't sing well. Daisy burst into tears and ran off the stage. Kitty could have danced a jig, she was so happy to see Daisy humiliated. *That is what she deserves*, Kitty thought and ran up to the stage to save Diablo's party.

Chio gave DJ Khaled a nod and he began playing Kitty's track. After singing the first verse of her song she told him to cut it off. "I need to let y'all know what real talent sounds like. I don't need any music," Kitty purred seductively. "This is for you, Diablo. Happy Birthday." She sang a beautiful rendition of *I Will Always Love You* better than Whitney's famous version of Dolly Parton's song. Diablo was impressed with Kitty's performance, but still cringing from the embarrassment of Daisy's snafu on stage. He wanted to go console her but decided to do damage control by opening the bar and giving away bottles of his best champagne. If he could get his guests drunk enough he hoped that they would forget the disaster he called his new artist.

Daisy ran into her girls by the bar where she sat drinking trying to drown her sorrows. "What do you wanna us to do to that cunt Kitty?" Anjel whispered in her best friend's ear as she hugged her tightly trying to console her.

"Cuz don't trip. We gonna whoop that hoe's ass for you." Mafia was furious at Kitty for sabotaging Daisy's set. The girls huddled around Daisy and led her to a room away from the packed party. Daisy wiped her tears and finally spoke.

"I want to kill that bitch."

"Oooooh lemme hit her up for you I got my jammy right here," squealed NellyPop gleefully, anxious to pop somebody with her two-shooter, she affectionately called her Jammy.

"No, I have my silencer. I will drop her as she leaves the stage. Nobody will even know what hit her," Sassy offered nonchalantly. She was a trained assassin and taking out Kitty would be child's play compared to the many people she had to murder in the Middle East.

"That sounds good. Let Sassy handle this one, NellyPop," ordered Mafia. Everyone agreed Sassy would shoot her as soon as she finished singing. They returned to the bar to make another toast as they waited for Kitty to sing the last note of her song. "Here's to the last song that bitch will ever sing." She raised her bottle and the girls followed suit. They each tapped their bottles together and took long swigs to the head in salute to Kitty's death.

CHAPTER 30

"Come with me to the bathroom, Anjel," Daisy said as she tugged on Anjel's arm.

"I need to go to wait up," NellyPop called after the girls. When they entered the bathroom Daisy broke down crying again.

"I wanted to impress Chio so bad and now I'm the joke of the night," sniffed Daisy. Anjel passed her some tissue and tried to console the distraught girl.

"If I was you I would put a hot one in that bitches ass for playing you like that," sneered NellyPop, while pulling out her jammy. Pointing it to the mirror she pretended to shoot.

"Let me see that," demanded Daisy.

"Here," NellyPop passed her the pearl-handled two shooter. NellyPop dug into her purse and produced a blunt filled with angel dust and weed.

"Gimme a pull," Daisy reached for the minty smelling blunt without bothering to ask what was in it. NellyPop smiled a dopey grin and passed Daisy the blunt. Daisy took a couple of pulls and passed it back and forth between the girls until they were all floating from the effects of the hallucinogenic "Imma go blast that skank right now for fucking up my life and stealing my man," slurred Daisy. She headed for the door moving in slow motion, she felt like she was walking or floating in space and could simply fly over the crowd and land in front of Kitty and blow her brains out. The thought was so funny to her she started laughing hysterically until the laughter turned to choked sobs.

Asia came into the room wilding out when she saw Daisy crying. "Man, fuck dat bitch shit. Go show that bird-ass motherfucking hoe who you be. You that bitch Daisy-Motherfucking-Jones, an OBG Ryder," shouted Asia, smacking five with Nelly. They were convincing Daisy to kill Kitty.

"Eh, y'all didn't Mafia say let Sassy take care of it?" said Anjel. She was paranoid and didn't really feel like being down on a body, she just wanted to go find her man and party. Daisy's drama was ruining her night. Her nerves were bad and she was high as fuck.

"I want to handle Kitty myself," said Daisy coldly. She felt indestructible and had a huge urge to see Kitty's brains smeared all over the floor. She ran out of the room and stormed through the party goers headed straight for Kitty. She spotted her target talking to Young Chio and Diablo. The sight of her nemesis talking to the two men enraged her. She felt electric sparks and pure hatred shoot through her brain and at the moment lost the presence of a sane mind. She had to destroy Kitty. She watched the girl flirt with the two men and they both loved it. Daisy pushed her way forward until she stood directly behind Kitty. She put the small gun against the back of her skull and fired one single shot. No one heard the muffled shot from the small weapon. Kitty slumped on Chio's chest. He thought she was hugging him and didn't realize that she was lying dead in his arms until he looked into Daisy's cold eyes. He saw pain and pure fury in her eyes.

"I loved you, bastard," mouthed Daisy, raising the gun to her own temple.

She pulled the trigger.

Tears streamed down her face when the lone remaining bullet cracked through her temple.

EPILOGUE

Mafia went postal at the scene of Daisy's suicide and grabbed Sassy's Glock and shot Young Chio six times, riddling his face with bullets. She was on the run for his murder, kidnapping and torturing Tela, and distribution of Narcotics.

Anthony and Casey were stunned by the horrific murders. Casey spit on Kitty's body and cried like a baby for Daisy and her sister. She was in anguish over her sister's incarceration and Daisy's death blew her mind.

Anthony was fucked up in the head over Daisy's suicide. All the anger he was holding against her went out the window. He only wished, he could hold her and tell her how much he loved her. If he had a chance, he would have waited for her and married her. He had to admit he loved her gold digging ass. But, unfortunately, it was too late.

Diablo was devastated by the incredible tragedy at his birthday party. He had no idea how much Daisy loathed Kitty and Chio and found the whole situation very confusing and sad. He went on to divorce Gazelle and found comfort in the arms of Miosha, the beautiful retired supermodel. Miosha thought that she had found the perfect man to settle down with and so did Tajil. Both she and Tajil met Diablo on that tragic night of Daisy's death. Tajil started seeing him on the down low and didn't know how to tell his boss that her man was his lover.

Labasia caught wind of the betrayal and told Miosha. She was in denial and refused to believe it until she set him up and actually caught Tajil and Diablo in bed together. All hell broke loose.

Ivy was sentenced to forty years in prison for murder and attempted murder charges. The government ran the kidnapping and identity theft concurrent with her murder felony. She was serving her sentence in the same prison Mistress was in and was reunited with her former partner in crime. She became very jealous of Mistress and her power in the jail as the leader of the OBG's so she started a renegade faction of the clique and went to war with Mistress, continuing to drip her poison behind the walls.

Anjel fell madly in love with Geechi and stopped dancing for his crew and insisted he treated her with respect. Her best friend Daisy killed herself over a jilted love and not being treated with the utmost respect and she vowed that she would not go out like that. She snapped out of all the bullshit and gave Geechi an ultimatum and of course he left her. As much as she loved him she let him go. She felt she had to honor Daisy's spirit and wouldn't let what happened to her friend be in vain. Anjel did a total three-sixty and went back to school. She graduated college with honors. She started seeing a therapist to deal with her father being her deceased mother's rapist and fell in love with her therapist. He was Japanese, handsome, and intrigued by her life story. They eventually got married and had a beautiful baby girl named, Daisy Kishimoto.

LETTER FROM *Mack Mama*

The tragic ending to this Drama comes as a surprise, but the reality is when you live in a fantasy world where materialism and manipulation is normal, the result is the player will face the consequences. He or 'she' in this matter will be played. Daisy lived her young life hard and fast; she was a gold digger who used men for material possessions and wealth. The saddest part of this story is that Daisy Jones learned to prey on men by her mother. Mama Jones lived vicariously through her daughter Daisy, sacrificing her youth and innocence to relieve her glory days or lack of. She trained Daisy to suppress her emotions and rely on calculation and trickery and the very emotion that she tried to make Daisy avoid ultimately destroyed her. The combination of lethal drugs and human emotions sent her to the brink of insanity.

Many young girls believe that oral sex isn't going all the way but that is a big misconception. Daisy Jones valued her virginity but degraded herself by substituting "oral" to get what she wanted from men. I know in Daisy's demise she wouldn't want to be remembered as the virgin who gave good head. There's no such thing as a halfway whore or halfway crook for that matter. Poison Ivy learned that the hard way. She was caught up in the fantasy of the glamorous hustling life style and began to believe that when she used other people's credit cards that she was spending her money causing her to get sloppy. She thought she was invincible and had no regard for human life. That fantasy doesn't last long. Soon the harsh reality sets in when the steel bars clang and she realized her freedom was gone. She was made to pay the price for all of her poisonous behavior.

Ultimately drugs played a major part in destroying Daisy. The lesson in that is simple: Drugs in any form alters your mind and enhances your emotions. So if you're in a bad mood it will take you to a ten and cause you to do things and react in a rage. The effects of drugs can be lethal emotionally, physically, and mentally.

There are so many lessons to be learned in this story and I wrote this to try and teach by example, because I lived so many parts of this book and I paid the price by losing my freedom. I talk to the youth in many schools around the country and I always use my life as an example on how to screw up, pay the price and ultimately get it right. I am "the" Original Bad Girl and if I can change my life than so can anyone. Find your talent and grind hard, focusing on nothing other than positive things and you will see results.

The drama will continue The O.B.G'S will continue to wreck havoc and Mistress will be home soon."*MISTRESS*"...the sequel to *Daisy Jones,* coming soon! If you want to know about the real life O.B.G read my autobiography "**Tales of an Original Bad Girl.**"

COMING SOON "MISTRESS" THE SEQUEL...the
drama continues...

ACKNOWLEDGEMENTS

I want to thank God in all of his infinite glory for giving me talent that in itself is a gift. Thanks for giving me the strength to persevere after all of the trials and tribulations I have experienced in my life.

I want to thank my best friend Queenie for always wanting more for me than I wanted for myself. I want to thank my sister Raquele for always believing in me and being the best lil sister on earth. I want to thank Kenya "Sparkles" Williams for supporting me and being my angel; love you to death. Thank you Cheryl "Goldie" Samuels for everything. I can always count on you, although we argue like cats and dogs, our bond is unbreakable. Love you to the death. Thanks for being you, Margaret "Poochie" Monroe. You have been down with me like four flats since the Albion days - love you.

I want to thank Alfred "Shaborn" Adams for embracing me as a fellow author and a friend; thanks for all the jewels that you gave me about the publishing game. Also for letting me sell your amazing books thru my company's catalog. You wanted nothing from the sales but for me to profit and for that unselfish act I pledge my love and loyalty forever.

Thank you Derrick "Bush" Hamilton for constantly rallying for my movement and in return I will do the same for yours. FREE "DERRICK HAMILTON", Sherm the Worm I love you and will always be there for you brother. Thank you Shaquell for the constant encouragement, love you bro. Miz you are such a talented writer, "G BANKS" is phenomenal as are all your books BISHOP the movie coming soon…

Thanks Monique "Mo Mo B" Bunting for your constant support and being you. I always say I wish I could sprinkle some Mo Mo B dust on all the women in the world; you are a real chick. Love you. You gave me an awesome interview on blog talk. Kareem "Berry" you are so sweet and a real gentlemen thanks for the constant support. Thanks Joe Ugly - I told you I would acknowledge you (smile) you gave me one of the best interviews on the net.

To Marina Mills I hope you are home by the time this book is released because you have been locked up far too long. I respect your constant battle for your freedom and love your loyalty and devotion to all things Mack Mama thanks for always repping your girl!

Keep your head up Joseph "Mighty" Jackson I miss you boo!

To Tom C. can't wait to you raise up outta your situation and shine like the star you are they ain't ready! Thanks to all of my supporters who purchased "*Tales of an Original Bad Girl*".

Special thanks to Latoya Foote, my rude gal, you soon come home! And Jamaica here we come. Thank you, Candy and St Croix Virgin Islands for showing me so much love. Thanks, to my blog talk folks for always showing me love, and giving me some dope interviews about my books. Thanks to Lisa Everts for having me on Street Soldiers Hot 97 what a great discussion "Gold diggers v Good Girls" S/O to Tionna Smalls and her #BossChickSorority, Special thank you to Dr .Michael Miller meeting you changed my perception of life your book was awesome and inspiring.

Last but not least I thank myself for never giving up regardless how many times I felt like getting my Daisy Jones on. I stayed focused and used my brains instead of my body.

It's hard when you are a sex symbol and famous in your mind and men tempt you with lavish gifts and money, to remain with your integrity intact. I love being an independent woman, because at the end of the day the struggle makes you appreciate the success so much more! (The sex symbol and famous in my mind reference is not conceit, but aware of my potential; don't confuse the two. I'm as humble as I can be; those who know me will vouch for that. So don't trip! ;-)

AFTERMATH

Booking info for speaking engagements, book signings, or performances contact mackmama1@gmail.com
Follow me on twitter @MackMama
"Like" me on facebook.com/mackmama
www.mackmamaworld.com
www.starstatuspublishing.com
www.blogtalkradio.com/mackmama

My incarcerated love ones send institutional check to
StarStatus Publishing
P.O Box 237
Derby Ct 06418

Send 10.95 plus 3.20 shipping and handling
Total 14.15

My autobiography "*Tales of an Original Bad Girl*" was my first book and since its arrival into the literary world has been a huge seller. If you want to know who I am and where I came from make sure you purchase TOAOBG from any online retailer or get the paperback version which includes 116 pictures, 52 which are in color.
TALES OF AN ORIGINAL BAD GIRL

Some say I was a female gangster, others say I was a professional thief. I say I am a woman who overcame the hell of 13 years in prison, domestic abuse and betrayal.
I witnessed my mother die from the AIDS virus when I was 16 and she was 36. As a result of that pain I became a vicious, bitter girl that lashed out violently, shooting or slashing anyone who betrayed me.
I was insane and suffered from the pain of abandonment; my mom chose drugs to cope with having the AIDS Virus and it ultimately destroyed me and herself.
I have since healed and matured into a career driven woman.
I am an entertainer, song writer, lyricist and business woman currently pursuing success in the literary field as an author and publisher. I share my story in hopes of helping the youth that are involved in the streets.

I want them to use my mistakes and learn from them and say "If Mack Mama can change so can I."

I also want the ladies and gentlemen who are released from prison to have their priorities in order and become entrepreneurs. If you can't get hired because of your criminal background, become your own boss; find what you are good at and capitalize off of it. God has blessed each of us with individual talent; use the time to find your gift.

Blessings—Mack Mama

To learn more about Mack Mama visit www.mackmamaworld.com

To purchase her autobiography visit www.starstatuspublishing.com

CPSIA information can be obtained
at www.ICGtesting.com
Printed in the USA
BVHW04s1740010518
514958BV00001B/28/P